PLAYING
A PART

PLAYING A PART

by DARIA WILKE

Translated from the Russian by MARIAN SCHWARTZ

ARTHUR A. LEVINE BOOKS

An Imprint of Scholastic Inc.

Library of Congress Cataloging-in-Publication Data

Wilke, Daria, author.
   [Shutovskoi kolpak. English]
   Playing a part / by Daria Wilke ; translated from the Russian by
Marian Schwartz. — [First American edition].
      pages cm
   Summary: Grishka has grown up in the closed world of a puppet
theater in Russia, but now that world seems to be falling apart — his
best friend needs an operation, financial difficulties are forcing people
out, his homosexual friend Sam, the jester, is leaving for Holland and
Grishka no longer knows what role he himself is playing.
   ISBN 978-0-545-72607-8 (hardcover : alk. paper) 1. Marionettes —
Juvenile fiction. 2. Puppeteers — Juvenile fiction. 3. Puppet
theater — Russia (Federation) — Juvenile fiction. 4. Gays — Russia
(Federation) — Juvenile fiction. 5. Identity (Psychology) — Juvenile
fiction. 6. Russia (Federation) — Juvenile fiction. [1. Marionettes —
Fiction. 2. Puppeteers — Fiction. 3. Puppet theater — Fiction.
4. Gays — Fiction. 5. Identity — Fiction. 6. Russia (Federation) —
Fiction.] I. Schwartz, Marian, translator. II. Title.
   PZ7.W648398Pl 2015
   [Fic] — dc23
                                                        2014012002

10 9 8 7 6 5 4 3 2 1   15 16 17 18 19

Originally published in Russian as *Shutovskoi kolpak*
by Samokat Publishing House, May 2013

First American edition, April 2015

Printed in the U.S.A.   23

Book design by Sharismar Rodriguez

To Mama and Papa,
without whom there would have been no theatrical childhood,
and to Stanley Burleson,
without whom there would have been no book

CONTENTS

"Make way, everyone, make way!
Step aside — here comes the Jester!"

I

THEATER KIDS

"GREASEPAINT makes everything easy as pie. Smear it on, and you feel confident. Think not? Just try it."

Over the makeup table, the light from the bulbs, which are as round as tree ornaments, is trembling. It's as if the old theater were going blind and squinting. Or winking at Sam all of a sudden, agreeing with him.

The theater smells sharp, like expensive cheese, from the open makeup box, and sweet, like a vanilla cookie, from the beige powder more than half gone in the tin with worn gilding.

Buskins — fancy leather boots with platform soles — swallow up Sam's feet.

"And buskins are for being taller onstage," Sam says, as if I didn't already know that. He's talking so matter-of-factly, as if nothing's happened — as if he hasn't just said he's leaving for good.

Sam's feet and toes, and the buskins too, suddenly smear and blur, and the light of the lamps over the makeup table dims, and something hot boils up in the corners of my eyes.

"What's wrong, Grish?"

Are you a man or what? my grandfather would say, and maybe he'd even be spitting mad. *Boys don't cry,* Anton would say. *You're being kind of weird.*

But you can do anything in the theater if you live there. Even cry, even if you're a boy.

Only I'm not going to cry — in front of him. I don't want Sam to know.

To know how upset I am.

Sam's face drifts, and now I can't see his wide eyebrows or his eyes, which he still hasn't made up for the evening performance.

"What's wrong?"

"Just a sec, Sam. . . ."

The theater opens all its doors wide and clears all its thresholds so I won't trip and hurt myself. My eyes can't see

2

anymore, but I know Sam is watching me go. And his jazz music races after me, tries to catch up, lift me over the earth, and help me run away. Sam always listens to jazz when he's putting on his makeup — softly, so he won't bother anybody.

There's just one place in the theater where you can cry without anyone seeing you. No one's going to pester you or start asking phony worried questions — "Who hurt you, Grish?" — and you won't have to snarl back — "I'll be the one hurting the first person who tries!"

Run past the old harpsichord with the fake candles, past the room where the big sets are kept — if the door is open, a chill will run down your legs — and slip past the women's dressing rooms and wardrobe.

And dart through a small door.

That's it. Now dive into the space between the slender-armed fairies and the puffy masks and sit down by the Jester. Now, even if your face is wet — it's okay.

I sit there hating everyone: Sam for leaving, that Holland place he's going to, my own mama and papa for not even trying to talk him out of it, the whole theater for not caring, and the people Sam can't bear any longer. And myself. I hate myself most of all because I'm crying like a baby, and I don't know how I'm going to go on.

The room where the puppets hang always smells of wood, glue, the folds of their brocade dresses, candy wrappers, and . . . miracles. The only people who come in here are the wardrobe people and the theater kids.

The theater kids are me and Sashok. The kids. That's what Albert Ilich, the theater's janitor, calls us.

I sit there feeling sorry for myself — until I'm sick of it. After all, it only *seems* as though I'm here alone. With the puppets, you're never alone. How can you feel sorry for yourself in a room full of people?

Masks and full-size puppets hang on a stand right by the door to make sure no strangers come in. The gray Mouse King with the evil eyes and shiny, bulging nose, and the pumpkin-headed fat man, and raggedy Baba Yaga. The puppets hang there with their colorful painted faces, silk ruches, and neat boots. They're all different; you won't find two exactly alike.

Occasionally someone's amazed that there are not just puppets, but people and masks on the puppet stage as well. A big puppet theater has room for everyone — marionettes, Punch and Judy, masks, and actors made up so you can't recognize them.

Papa calls this "combined theater."

In the back, forgotten by all, hang my favorites — the puppets from shows now gone from the stage. Sad Losharik the horse, the Little Fairy with her slender arms and marvelous dress. The Tin Soldier looks sternly at you, standing at attention. The pot-bellied Mouse from *All Mice Love Cheese* looks on sympathetically. The Jester in his multicolored cap gives you an amused look.

Oh, the Jester! With all that crying, I completely forgot. Soon, the Jester will be mine!

Today Lyolik said they're going to decommission *The Glass Slipper.*

All the shows get decommissioned sooner or later — and so do the puppets.

I always dreamed of getting the Jester. Because *I* am a jester. I tease the teachers in school. I talk to them in voices. I make jokes about the other kids. I'm Grishka the Pest.

To other people, I'm a jester.

Like him, just like him. Sam is the Jester.

That's what I always think when I take the Jester's hand. His palm is smooth and cozy, and it rests quietly in mine. Then the puppet tilts his head archly, so you can see his hooked nose with the bump, and he winks at me — "I do declare!" — and his eyes are clear, as if he hasn't been waiting here, backstage on the puppet stand, for a good hour to go to work.

"Sam, you're on!" Vika, the assistant director, usually shouts in her terrible, loud whisper, downward and sideways, when they're performing *Slipper*.

And now Sam runs, throwing the netting from his special black theater costume over his head, and grabs the Jester by its controller — and immediately the Jester's sinew-strings pull tight. His arm jerks awkwardly, and his feet step out from the wings to a full house. At that moment, the Jester actually becomes a little less alive — he becomes an ordinary marionette on an ordinary stage. The scraps on the Jester's cap flutter — apple red, cornflower blue, and gooseberry purple.

But the Jester laughs and sings — and Sam dissolves into him. The Jester hides Sam, as if he had never existed and there are only the black eyes and rascally smiles of the Jester, sculpted once upon a time by Lyolik, the theater's puppet master.

◆

Sam's name is actually Semyon. But one day someone said "Sam," and the name stuck. Because *Semyon*, though quite pretty, somehow isn't very theatrical. Even when you see him offstage in the evening, after the show at the stage door, he's obviously a Sam. Handsome and stylish. The scarf wound nonchalantly around his neck, the turned-up collar on his flight jacket, the checked velvet trousers, and the round-toed boots. Sam's the whole package. Onstage he doesn't change in the slightest.

No, actually, he changes before he goes onstage. When I was little, I tried to be next to Sam when it happened. I tried not to miss the moment when he appeared from the dressing room to run to the stage entrance.

I couldn't tear my eyes away from him, trying to catch the moment Sam transformed into someone else.

But I always missed that split second when he crossed some invisible line on the floor of the passage leading from the makeup room to the curtain's black labyrinth.

All I saw was that someone else had taken up residence in Sam, that he was now moving completely differently. Even his palms, even the strong back of Sam's head and his flexible shoulders, seemed alien, like modeling clay. So changed I didn't recognize them.

It was always awful for me to see Sam step out of the backstage shadow into the light of the stage. I wanted to reach out and touch him to be convinced that it was really him.

Onstage, his face melts into hundreds of other faces — young and old, soft and sharp. Onstage, he knows how to walk softly, stealthily, like a large, unpredictable cat, or angularly and clumsily, as if each step costs him inhuman effort. He knows how to fly onto the stage, barely touching the floor, swathed in black fabric, as if he himself weighs nothing. He knows how to make everything around him beautiful, and even in the ugliest makeup he takes your breath away.

Each time he plays a devil in one of the shows, I freeze on the spot. Because Sam spins on his heels, spins as deftly as a top, spreads his arms, and throws his head back. The hem of his scarlet frock-coat unfurls like a flower — and then suddenly he stops and laughs — a deep laugh, from his very core, that seems to make the air around him tremble; his laughter seeps into the wings, into everyone sitting in the audience, and into me. It seeps, it works its way right inside you, and everything inside you warms up, like after you drink tea with honey. His laughter runs hot through your veins, shoots straight through you, as if it were seeping all the way down to your toes. It presses my feet down, grounding me permanently.

That's what Sam can do.

After all, Sam is the Jester. That I know. The most genuine, most super, most perfect Jester. The Jester is his puppet. His role, which he plays better than anyone.

When I asked to have the puppet, I didn't know about Holland.

I didn't know Sam would be leaving soon for good.

But now I'm awfully glad I asked for the Jester. This way I'll have something to remember him by.

♦

The Jester is Lyolik's very best puppet. Even Lyolik says so.

Lyolik's a jester too, of course.

He was here before I was born. Before all the puppets were born. He must be a hundred years old and he's seen it all, so there's a story behind every word he says.

The door to the theater workshop — to Lyolik's — is always open. It can be noisy and crazy outside, but cross his threshold and you're in another, magical world.

As soon as you step on the cracked but sturdy steps leading steeply down — and stoop a little because there's an old vaulted ceiling overhead — you catch the smell of fresh paper, glue, linden and birch shavings, the chocolate candies he always has here for tea, sharply sour paint — and hay, for whatever reason.

Lyolik is always sitting there, on a tall chair cleverly positioned so that he can see both the people rushing through the Moscow streets outside the window, hurrying about their business, and the wide-open workshop doors beyond which lies the actors' perpetual pandemonium.

Lyolik smiles broadly, from ear to ear; his mouth works independently; his brow is furrowed and ripples in waves; his glasses slip all the way down to the tip of his big, hooked nose; and, leaning over a puppet head, he looks like a fairy-tale hunchback, with hands hewn from an oak stump. All his fingers are different, as if some inept someone, in making a puppet, had stuck on fingers from hand puppets and china puppets, from rag-doll Punches and antique wooden nutcrackers. His hands look clumsy — but looks can be deceiving. No one can carve the fingers for Cinderella like Lyolik, or draw the squinting eyes of Puss in Boots, or glue the hairs to the Tin Soldier's brows like Lyolik anymore.

◆

Earlier today we were sitting in his workshop blowing on our tea. That was when Lyolik said *The Glass Slipper* was going to be decommissioned. Before New Year's.

"But where will the puppets go?" I asked. "Where will Cinderella and the snooty Queen Mother go? Where will the Fairy and the Jester go?"

Lyolik just shrugged. "Where they usually do."

The actors take the decommissioned puppets home. For instance, at home, in our hall closet, we have the bald King

Midas in his crimson chiton, and some large masks: a granny with glasses and a mousy-colored cap, and the little blue-eyed girl from *The Three Bears*.

Later, when I saw our artistic director, Kolokolchikov, Olezhek Kolokolchikov, in the passage, I nearly yelled, "Can I take the Jester when they decommission him?"

For some reason I knew that the Jester absolutely, just absolutely, had to stay with me.

"Sure," Olezhek said distractedly, not even looking in my direction. "Sure, certainly, take it."

That's how I got permission to take the Jester.

◆

"Are you there? Why are you hiding?"

I knew Sashok would find me, even in the puppet room.

She stands there staring at me with her big, round eyes.

"What were you doing? Crying? Are you a total idiot or something?" Sashok is my godsister.

Lyolik says there's no such thing, but for me there is.

Sashok's papa is my godfather and they christened us together. (We were eight years old, so I remember it well.)

I always wanted to have a sister, and I like thinking that Sashok is my sister, even though our parents aren't related; they're just friends.

If anyone at school calls me Grishka the Clown, Grishka the Pest, they clearly don't know what Sashok can be like. If you want to know who's the pest . . .

But right now I wish I could disappear, and I get a horrible feeling, as if my cheeks were filling with boiling water, and even the skin under my hair turns red.

"Grishka, the Maiden Red," Sashok says, and the right corner of her mouth twitches a little, like one of Lyolik's puppets. She immediately looks away, as if red-faced me is more than she can bear.

"Why were you crying?"

If you saw us on the street, from behind, for instance, you could easily have trouble telling which one's the boy and which one's the girl.

Sashok's hair is cut like a boy's. She's angular and has big ears, and when she walks she swings her arms briskly. Whereas I don't like to run; I feel like almost dancing when I walk. "You ball of fluff," Sashok sometimes says affectionately, reaching for my hair as if it really were dandelion fluff just about to fly away, and not the shaggy, curly head of hair I got from who knows where.

It's as if Sashok is proud not to have braids or silly princess dolls.

"Mama and Papa, thank you very much for bringing me

home from the hospital in a green blanket!" Sashok likes to say, stressing that all that pink and blue stuff has nothing to do with her.

I love her very much because she doesn't dress up like a princess and doesn't ask her parents to buy her a dress the pink of the sticky cotton candy at the amusement park. And because she's easy to talk to about anything — it's like talking to someone like you, not a girl. And I probably even like that she's a pest. She doesn't mean any harm; that's just the way she is.

"Come on, spill!"

Sashok won't back down, I know. So it's best just to come clean.

"Sam said he's going to Holland. Forever. To work there, and live there, for good."

"I see," Sashok says, and she sits down beside me on a wooden step.

She doesn't say anything for a while.

Then she takes a deep breath — the smell of candy wrappers, shavings, and brocade puppet costumes — and she comes out with this: "And I'm going to have an operation. After my birthday."

Sashok has something wrong with her heart, some syndrome whose name I can never remember. "Nothing terrible, just palpitations," she's said. But they told her once that an operation might be necessary if the palpitations started to bother her.

Sashok's had the syndrome since she was a kid; that's why her lips are often totally blue, as if she's smeared them with watercolors as a joke.

I always wondered what the palpitations were like.

That they could bother her.

"Well, it's like you've got a crazed bird locked up inside you and it's beating its wings in there but can't get out," Sashok said one day, without even the whisper of a smile.

I've always thought operations were very scary. I've never been in a hospital — as if, like the Jester, I'm not made of the same stuff as everyone else.

But Sashok's another matter. She's not me. She's fearless. Or maybe she just pretends she is.

"They tell me the operation's safe, nothing serious. But for some reason I keep thinking that's not true."

She glances at me, briefly, as if she doesn't want me to see her eyes.

"I'm afraid of the anesthetic. At night I lie in my bed and wonder, what if I don't wake up tomorrow? Then I don't want to fall asleep, so I try not to close my eyes, as long as I can stand it. And then — there it is — I don't want to, but

I fall asleep. And the next night it's the same thing all over again."

I don't know what to say. If Sashok admits she's scared, that means she's very scared. Which is why, just to cheer her up, I blurt out, "Guess what? They're going to decommission *The Glass Slipper* soon, and you can take any puppet you want."

I think she'll take Cinderella, or maybe the Queen. They're so beautiful, sometimes you feel like squinting because your eyes can't take that much beauty.

But this is Sashok, after all.

Her eyes glitter. Because, of course, I really am a complete fool.

"That means I can ask for the Jester!" Sashok exclaims. "It's no stupid, girly puppet," she says after thinking about it, as if she's continuing to argue with someone, "like the kind you'd ask for on your birthday."

Sashok's birthday is December 31, and she never invites me to celebrate it because she never has a party. It's rare she gets presents, since it's New Year's, after all. Up to the day itself, her parents work the holiday shows — just like mine. The holiday season, and all that.

"So they really might give me the Jester," Sashok says, and she cocks her head like a magpie.

Theater kids — it's not just me and Sashok, after all. It's the grown-ups too, I suddenly realize. Absolutely everyone who lives in the theater: Lyolik, Sam, Mama Carlo, Maika on lights, and even Nina Ivanovna, the fat lady at the snack counter with pink lips and blond hair whipped up like a fancy cake. And we may be all one another has. The theater too — we have that. The theater's always here. Everyone can count on a piece of the theater — that's a certainty. That's honest.

Sam would surely have done the same, I decide.

The theater's creaking stairs sigh: It's the right thing to do.

I'll give Sashok the Jester. How can I not?

II

THE PUPPET GOD

"IF there is a puppet god, then it's Lyolik," Sam said once, a long time ago. Said it and forgot it. But I remember to this day.

Every time I see Sam in Lyolik's workshop, I think that if Lyolik's a god, then Sam worships him, for sure. If Lyolik needs wood brought up from downstairs or blocks or boards from the garage, Sam runs to do it like a little boy, as if the theater has no stagehands. If Lyolik suddenly and unexpectedly needs glue from the store, Sam darts off: "I'll be quick!" With Lyolik, he's not calm, grown-up Sam anymore. He's someone like me or Sashok.

Once every two weeks Sam takes Lyolik to the Home for Veterans of the Stage to visit some old puppet master who used to work in our theater and taught Lyolik how to make puppets.

Like today. You can get so much done between morning rehearsals and the evening performance.

I run to the workshop so I won't miss them, so they won't up and leave without me. Every day now, all the time, it feels as though Sam is slipping away, as though tomorrow I'll wake up and he'll be gone. Never to return.

To get to Lyolik's, I have to dash past the stage entrance, past the tiny door to the long, narrow passage under the stage, and past the smoking room and the dressing rooms on the second floor. "One day you'll knock me down, Grisha!" Vinnik the actress shouts. She's come out of the dressing room wearing a Bordeaux-red velvet dress with a crinoline petticoat and a violet-tinted gray wig — holding a cigarette at arm's length and squinting helplessly without her glasses. Not very likely! I won't knock her over. I'm no fool. If you grow up in the puppet theater, slipping through the crack between the crinoline and the wall is child's play.

"Grisha, how's about your tea?" Mama Carlo asks, or rather hollers, from her doorway, immediately answering for me. Mama Carlo is Lyolik's sister. She's top boss in the theater workshops, though you wouldn't think so if you saw her. Mama Carlo looks like the pot-bellied grenadier from an old show: her hair tousled like a cap, suspenders the color of autumn leaves holding up her too-short trousers. A giant of a grenadier. An almost-granny wearing trousers to her ankles. Only she would have the nerve to wear clothes like that.

Sure, lots of other people work in the workshops too, but all I see is Lyolik and Mama Carlo, as if they were there alone.

Mama Carlo is perpetually behind because theater workshops are never calm. Sometimes she's so behind, the hair on her head grows out too fast for her to notice. Today, for instance, half her head is gray. All of a sudden you look at Mama Carlo and it looks as though someone ran a sharp razor around the middle, and on one side it's very gray, and on the other there's the black dye she likes to use to doll herself up.

On the other hand, she always has time for tea — tea with Sam, or with me, or with anyone who turns up on her doorstep.

Tea with Mama Carlo is special. She brews it in an antique teapot with firebirds on the sides. That's probably why it's so fragrant, so honey-brown. It steams, and the steam draws patterns on the tea's surface as if it were a small pond, not a cup.

With the tea she serves Lyolik's Candy Puppet Show.

Lyolik pushes a worn fool's cap, made for some old show, toward me and Sam, looks over his glasses, and winks — and the Candy Puppet Show begins. Each time, Sam seems tickled pink, as if he didn't know it all by heart. He smiles, and even his eyebrows and nose smile, and a dimple you didn't see before appears on his left cheek.

The game is, you have to reach into the hat and pull out a piece of candy — that one's yours. It's more fun that way. Everyone's long since forgotten which candies they filled the cap with a hundred years ago.

Lying around on the table are twisted wires, hinges, screws, and dowels — so you have to be careful what you eat! (Dowels are the little wooden pins that get hidden deep inside the puppet and make its eyes move and its mouth talk.)

Right by the full cups of tea are some round fox heads. Lyolik was just rubbing them with his crooked fingers to make arcs in the modeling clay over the brows and to make sure there are clefts on their noses.

"Well, shall we get a move on?" Sam stands up and wraps his long scarf around his neck.

He flies up the stairs, but Lyolik is in no hurry to put

his arms in the sleeves of his gray fall coat and take the string bag full of bananas and Mama Carlo's savory pie out of the refrigerator that's right in the middle of the workshop ("Proper workshops must have their own refrigerators!").

"Do your parents know?" Mama Carlo suddenly remembers to ask when I've nearly run off.

"You tell them, okay?" I shout to her from the doorway, and Mama Carlo gestures vaguely.

"Going far?" Sashok always turns up at the wrong time, I think — and am immediately ashamed.

Lyolik and Sam have gone on ahead, to the door, to Sam's car, and I really don't want Sashok tagging along. It's not that I don't want her to go per se. I just want to have Sam to myself. And Lyolik. Sam is leaving for good soon, and Sashok will always be here and we'll still have chances to go everywhere.

"Back soon," I lie, and I slip out, not looking at her, to the passage, past Albert Ilich, the gray-browed janitor, who's drinking tea and staring at a small TV.

The instant you walk out the stage door, you're in Moscow. As long as you're in the theater, there doesn't seem to be anywhere else but the theater. No stores with people busily putting milk in carts, no square and round loaves of bread, no flashing traffic lights, no racing cars. In the theater

23

you don't even need windows, because the theater is the theater and that's all you need.

In the theater there is no fall or winter, no morning or night — it's always its own season and day. The theater season, the theater day.

But walk through the stage door and there you are in Moscow — and it's fall.

Fall means the theatrical season has only just begun.

Fall means a drift of leaves next to the door: lemon yellow, rusty brown, strawberry red.

"Hurry up!" Sam shouts in the distance. I can't hear him but I can see his lips moving and his arm gesturing. Then I forget about the leaves and dash for the car — and the fall wind whistles in my ears and the Moscow streets roar.

Lyolik rides with dignity, the bag with the pie in his lap. Occasionally he turns to look at something out the window, and then from the backseat I can see that in profile he looks even more like the Jester, with his hooked nose and shaggy gray eyebrows.

◆

When I was little, one day I suddenly realized I didn't know where old actors went. I got very scared. Someone was just here, he went out onstage, he was a part of every day, you watched him magically transform himself to play a part, he shone, and all of a sudden — *zap!* — he was gone, vanished, like the puppets from decommissioned shows. And no one said anything, as if no one actually knew what happened to him.

I asked my mama, "So where do they disappear to? Where do the actors go who aren't working in the theater anymore?"

"Here and there," my mama said. "Some just go to live quietly with their grandchildren and water the cucumbers at their place in the country, and some move to the Home for Veterans of the Stage."

I always thought that the Home was a kind of palace where the rooms were furnished with antique vases and fancy lamps, and old men and women with hairdos like in the costume dramas lived. They sat at round tables and drank tea from saucers with fanciful monograms on the bottom, next to walls hung top to bottom with engravings and yellowed photographs in fancy frames.

The Home is somewhere in the forest. That I know for certain. Sometimes we would ride by it on the bus. And then — at the exact same place each time — my papa would say significantly, "And over there is the Home for Veterans of the Stage." You can't see it through the trees, even in winter when all the leaves have fallen, and I've always wanted so badly to take just a peek at the "palace."

Sam parks the car and we start off through the autumnal park. It's resoundingly quiet, as if we've fallen into another time, another world. There is a smell of acrid smoke: We can't see who, but someone is burning fallen leaves in the long lanes.

"Now don't you go running off," Lyolik grumbles at Sam when Sam takes his string bag, even though it isn't heavy.

All of a sudden, though there isn't any wind, the plane trees shower us with translucent, pale yellow leaves. First, one falls slowly and cautiously. Then, spinning, another three, and then the black, wet-looking trunks are engulfed in a yellow swirl of leaves so big there's no seeing where it stops. There's no more ground, just amber leaves shuddering and shifting underfoot.

And in the lane, in that yellow shower of leaves, an old woman appears. Never in the world would I have thought she was an old woman if she hadn't been leaning on a cane. I'd have thought she was a ballerina because of her perfect posture — as if something inside her were forcing her to stretch tautly — and her smoothly combed hair.

She's walking majestically down the lane, and around her dance mute and weightless plane tree leaves. She doesn't turn around when she hears steps, and only when we catch up with her does she glance at Lyolik and Sam, bow her head in formal greeting, and quietly say, "To see Efimovich? That's good."

As if she were the queen of the Home. The prima ballerina who shall always be the prima, even with a cane, even if her once-blue eyes are faded and each hair on her head is stitched with silver.

Turns out, the Home isn't a palace at all.

It's just a typical boarding house outside Moscow, with tall windows, I think, disappointed. A boarding house, not a palace.

Inside, it's strangely quiet, as if no one actually lives in the Home.

And it has a smell. A strange smell. A school smells of cafeteria food and shoe bags. Dressing rooms, of powder and makeup. Home, of warmth and Mama's jasmine perfume. But the Home has a strange smell — sort of sweet, too sweet, sort of as if you'd poked your nose into a laundry hamper.

The smell opens my eyes to the fact that there are pieces of parquet missing from the floor here and there where dirt has accumulated; that lacy, worn-out wallpaper dangles in the corners; and that the flowers at the hall window have dried out, curled up, and turned brown, nearly black.

On the second floor it suddenly gets noisy. *Boom boom boom* — drums are booming somewhere, many voices are producing something unimaginable, and saxophones are wailing.

Sam laughs and knocks so loudly I think I'll go deaf.

Then again. And again — because no one hears him.

"Get lost already!" someone inside hollers.

I shrink. Why did we come if he's going to attack us? What if he's out of his mind?

"Go away!" The door clicks, rumbles, and swings open.

A band bursts out of the room and knocks us off our feet, and I think I'd better hang on to the doorframe.

On the threshold stands a skinny little man who reminds me of a turtle. His head is perfectly bald, and wrinkles seem to have gathered on the very top of it.

His eyebrows look like two hooks, as if someone has taken them off some puppet and attached them to his face.

He rushes to embrace Lyolik and Sam and then holds his hand out to me in a dignified way, as if I'm some sort of big shot. A minute later he's forgotten all about me and is back at his table.

"Lyonechka, no, look, look at the controller they sent me from Germany. No, really, look what they're doing, look!"

This is the first time I've ever heard anyone call Lyolik "Lyonechka."

He runs to us from the table — which is buried under piles of patterns and sketches, new and old, and even ones so ancient the paper has yellowed and frayed — and back.

He points to the patterns and shows Lyolik his wonderful new controller.

"Look at how they reinforce the leg yoke. Can you imagine how it moves?"

He exclaims, he tries to outshout the horns and saxophones, he hops, he barely stands still for a second, and then he jumps up, runs to the cupboards, gets out some old puppets, and shows us things. He speaks breathlessly, as if he hasn't spoken in a hundred years and now has finally decided to open his mouth.

From the way Lyolik looks at him, you can tell that this is the true puppet god.

Sam turns off the music and neatly folds the plans scattered over the table — so there will be somewhere to put the pie. Out of his pocket he takes a shiny new box with foreign letters curling over the lid and holds it out to Efimovich, who grabs the package like a child, with both hands, and gleefully eviscerates it — and instantly the room is filled with the sharp smell of tobacco. He stuffs his nostrils, gives his head a silly wag, screws up his eyes, winks at Sam, sneezes like a cat, and stuffs his nose with more tobacco. He ends up with two tobacco tracks down his lip, but he pays them no mind and has no intention of wiping them off.

There's a delicate knock at the door. Efimovich frowns and freezes, as if newcomers from the Home might bring disaster to his room, which is hung with marionettes, rod puppets, masks, and posters.

"Well, come in, who's there?"

The ballerina from the lane floats through the door — now without a cane, carrying a tray with steaming cups. For everyone.

"Tea," she says, and inclines her head on her swanlike neck, which does not seem to bend at all. "I thought you would like some tea."

Even queens bow to puppet gods, I think, as the ballerina, her back perfectly straight, walks out the door.

"She looks after me," Efimovich says proudly, and he raises his hook-brows.

With obvious delight, he cuts himself a piece of pie, and you can see right away that the cabbage inside is bright green, and you can smell Mama Carlo's trademark filling. Sam looks at Efimovich's hands, and Efimovich catches his look.

"Oh, no." Sam takes a step back in fright. "I'm not going to. This is for you."

"And I won't give you any." Efimovich squints craftily, and his eyes drown in webs of infinite wrinkles. "Lyonechka, of course you'll eat!"

He holds out a piece each to me and Lyolik.

"I thought the actors in the Home were like the decommissioned puppets," I blab, and am instantly ready to burn up from shame. My head feels as though it has been plunged into a hot bath. Now Efimovich is sure to be mad.

But he only bursts out laughing.

"Decommissioned! No one can decommission you until you decommission yourself. As long as I have my puppets and plans, there is no retirement or old age, and death will have to wait outside."

Now he's giggling and cackling loudly.

"When I finally retire, I'll come join you," Lyolik says as we're leaving, and you can tell this is their ritual, that he says this every time. "I'm not going to stay at home."

My heart sinks.

Lyolik seems like he's a hundred years old, and he just got his pension, but he's still working anyway. He often says he's going to work "until they carry me out feet first." I hope they don't take Lyolik out soon. Otherwise, who am I going to visit in the workshops when I'm sad? Jesters can be sad too.

But if he talks to Efimovich about retiring every time, and about going to the Home, does that mean he really is planning to come here?

It's quiet in the corridor again — as if the only life here is on the other side of the door, where the drums are booming away again and puppets hang on the walls.

"You don't believe that yourself," Sam says when we go outside. "You just say that. What do you need a charity home for?"

"A lot you know," Lyolik answers angrily. "A lot you know! This is like a resort — you just stay until your life is over."

"The only good thing to do in a resort is relax," Sam says stubbornly and quietly. "You need a real home. A charity home is just charity, after all."

And all of a sudden I understand. What an idiot I am. Of course, this is a charity home. An honest-to-goodness charity home. And I've been picturing some kind of palace. Or boarding house.

◆

The autumn breeze quietly turns off the lights in the big city, the way the lamps get turned down in the theater, one by one: the heavy chandelier, then the sconces in the balconies. And then, cautiously, as if testing their powers, the lights are lit onstage. Phantasmal, fanciful. The kitchen and nursery windows we pass flicker with magical lamps; each window reveals its own scene, its own theater. The autumn moon shines like a dim floodlamp in the inky blue sky.

Only when Sam cuts the engine and says, "We're here!" do I realize that neither one of them has spoken a word the whole time. Sam and Lyolik have been silent all the way to the theater, as if they are mad at each other.

When you go back inside the theater, it always feels like going home; everything is familiar and understandable. Outside, people have donned their masks and are scurrying home after work. But in the theater, masks are just masks, not an alternate face. Everything is done honestly. You don't have to pretend here, even though you'd think it would be just the opposite.

Lyolik wanders toward the workshops, where he's always supposed to be during the evening performance. Because only he can repair any puppet. If something breaks, they rush it over to Lyolik during intermission, and in fifteen minutes he's figured out how to fix it. Or to bandage it up so it can perform the second act.

Right now, Sam is about to start singing; today he has *The Nutcracker*, where he sings. Better not bother him. I should bug off, even though I'm dying to sit next to Sam and listen to him sing.

I love the shows where Sam gets to sing and doesn't hide behind a curtain most of the time.

Because that's when the mystery begins. Sam plays his voice like an organ, choosing each note with care. His voice gradually fills the entire hall, to the farthest corner. It twists and turns like an invisible scroll. It breathes and vibrates.

They are all busy — and I still haven't checked on the Jester or taken my run through the theater. I need to check on everyone. Then the evening will go the way it should and I can just sit in the dressing room and eat cake from the theater snack bar and do my homework for tomorrow.

Sashok isn't in the theater. I mean, she's here somewhere, of course, but I can't find her. She isn't with Mama Carlo or in the dressing rooms. In the theater, everything is out in the open and everything is hidden from those who can't picture how it's arranged. I know that sooner or later Sashok will jump out like a devil from a snuffbox. But if I search for her specially, nothing will come of it.

I run through the theater, and the hallway floor flies under my feet like a turntable.

"Careful on the curves, kid." Olezhek rustles reproachfully.

He's turned the corner at just the wrong time. When he

walks, he kicks his feet like a fly rubbing its legs — not like the artistic director of a Moscow theater passing through his realms — and flaps his short little arms. To Kolokolchikov, everyone is "kid": Lyolik, Mama, Papa, Sam, even the wrinkly janitor, Albert Ilich. That's why I feel sorry for Oleg Borisovich — no one takes him seriously. Everyone just calls him Olezhek, whether because only recently he was an actor like everyone else or because of those "kids."

The wings, backdrops, and gratings are the borders of my territory. I run past them so fast the wind whistles in my ears. The house is boring, and so is the lobby. Farther on, past my border checkpoint, on the left, in the dark passageway behind the stage, there's a little hidden door covered in foam rubber. You have to creep through it, bent over. I run down the narrow passage to the space under the stage and watch everyone getting ready for the Mouse King's entrance. A mask with lots of evil mouse heads is hanging on a hook, awaiting its hour.

Then I run like mad back down the underground passage and then up the spiral staircase, past the sound man. And into the booth with Maika, the lighting tech, where I plop down on the worn-out chair in front of the huge console — it looks like a spaceship — and watch, holding my breath, as the Mouse King emerges from underground, as if from a dark abyss. If Maika lets me, I can slowly move the lever on the console and watch the abyss blaze up with devilish light. You're almost God because your hand is resting on that tiny little lever.

Maika always smells of strong coffee.

All my life there's been a green mug next to the console, so by now I imagine Maika has thick, black coffee running through her veins instead of blood.

"I knew it! I knew you'd be here!" Sashok shouts in a triumphant whisper. You'd think I was the one who disappeared, as if I'd been swallowed alive by the storage room. "Let's go! Hurry up! Before the criminal escapes!"

She drags me to the balcony, and I don't even have a chance, like I usually do, to look down through the floodlights' safety nets, down into the dark and seemingly lifeless house, and then look up to see Misha the sound man sitting in the little window on the left and wave to him.

"Basically," Sashok reports near the dressing rooms, "there's a stranger there, downstairs. A criminal. And he's probably looking to swipe our puppets."

Everything in the theater is ours. The puppets, the old harpsichord in the hallway, the stiff, lacquered wigs on the wig stands.

Sashok likes to exaggerate. She likes to turn everything into a drama, so naturally I don't believe there are any criminals. But I go, because if Sashok says, "Let's go," you'd have to be suicidal not to. You can't not go if Sashok's decided you absolutely have to go somewhere.

Downstairs means the Little Stage. Nearly in the basement. You have to take a steep black staircase, and you have to get used to the low light and huddle because everything's so dark. And there really is a stranger in that low light. He's standing right there by the puppets that are hung up for tomorrow's matinee.

He's skinny and nimble, like a scraggly grass snake. He has an earring and a tattoo that covers one whole chicken-wing arm and a neat little goatee. I dislike him right away. Because he's holding the Jester. My Jester.

"Who gave you permission to take the Jester?" Sashok screams. If she screams, that means even she's not altogether sure that she's not going to get slapped. "Who are you, anyway?"

"What's it to you?" the guy asks, in an almost threatening way.

"It's a lot to us," Sashok replies in the same tone. "We live here."

The guy hesitates but finally says, "I'm the new puppet master."

III

PARTY JACKET

MY grandfather wouldn't have guessed anything if Sam hadn't put on his party jacket. When he puts on his party jackets, even a dimwit could guess.

Because Sam's party jackets are bright green with black satin lapels or red sparkly ones. Today he puts on a jacket in a navy floral pattern.

It's a handsome jacket.

"Papa, this is Sam," Mama says happily when she introduces them to each other. She says it as if half of Moscow is wearing jackets like that and it's not anything special.

My grandfather straightens up with a jerk, gawks, and looks at me — and I nod, as if to say, *Yes, that's Sam, nothing you can do about it* — and then back at Sam.

And Sam smiles at him — broadly, joyfully.

Sam smiles and it's impossible not to smile back because Sam glows like a furnace going full blast.

My grandfather says, "Mmm hmm," and that's it. Not even a "pleased to meet you," or something else polite like you're supposed to say in these circumstances.

When we're alone in the dressing room — him and me, because I have to show him where he can change and leave his things — my grandfather says with disgust, "You're always going on about your friend, your friend! I thought he was a regular fellow, but he's . . . he's just a queer." And he frowns. "A queer," he repeats disdainfully.

It's as if I've been punched in the chest and my whole insides have contracted and squeezed in self-defense.

Because I want to tell my grandfather that Sam is the very best actor and now he's leaving and I feel terrible. Sam can turn into a hundred different people onstage. Sam took Lyolik to the Home for Veterans of the Stage. Sometimes Sam seems like an entire world, much better than the rest of the world. I want to — and can't.

Because my grandfather said "queer."

At first I was really happy they'd be celebrating my Mama's premiere at the theater instead of at home.

At home, once the guests have arrived, everything falls into place and Mama and Papa play the radiant hosts. But all morning, before the guests' arrival, our apartment is an absolute madhouse.

Someone always forgets to buy something, and my parents spend a long time arguing over who should go to the store. And, of course, it's Papa who always goes — "because you're the man. Are you a man, or what?"

He goes, slamming the door as hard as he can, but just before that he shouts, "You don't treat me like a human being here! I'm a . . . I'm a . . . I'm like Cinderella!"

Then he calls from the store ten times, probably stopping at every shelf. At first Mama smiles sympathetically, but by the fifth call her voice gets steely, and by the tenth she's shouting into the receiver, "I can never count on you!" and she throws the phone on the couch in the kitchen, as if it were the phone's fault that she can't count on Papa and that she ever married him.

Later we'll sit in a circle around a big bowl to chop things up for salads, each with our own cutting board. It's not too bad if my parents are just quarreling. If, for instance, Mama shouts, "Lazy goat! Brute!" and Papa goes crazy and throws his knife at the table so that it hits the edge of the plate of parings and it's smashed to pieces — well, that gives him a scare and he quiets down.

It's good if that's what happens. It can be worse. Like last time — when Mama was stirring mayonnaise into the salad and in the heat of the moment Papa said something stupid. They stood there yelling at each other, and then Mama outshouted Papa: "You and all your guests can get out!" and she hurled the big bowl of salad at the wall.

I have no idea where she got the strength to do that. The salad flew all over the kitchen — onto the walls, the ceiling, the refrigerator, and the shelves — and there was even some mayonnaise-y shredded carrot on the windowsill, and potato, and egg yolk bits, and peas on the floor.

When something like that happens, they quickly realize they've gone too far with the drama ("They've screwed up big-time," Sashok would say), and they make up then and there. They crawl around on the floor, pick up the peas and potato, wash the windows, and nudge each other with their elbows as if to make sure they're still there. They hug and fuss — "Give me that rag, please." "I'll shut the window so you don't get a draft."

They're so nice to look at, perfect lovebirds. As if they'd just been married yesterday.

No, I really have first-rate parents. No one else in school has anything like them.

Who else has a mama who can make you laugh, or who can suddenly start talking in the voice of the rabbit from the kiddie show? And then answer as the hedgehog. Or the fox. And go on and on, squeaking, then barking, then snuffling and snorting, until you're having so much fun you start laughing like a nut?

Having actors for parents is like having a birthmark in the most obvious and unsuitable place. There's nothing you can do about it. Everyone notices, but you shouldn't complain.

Basically, it was good they decided to celebrate the premiere at the theater and not at our house. That's what I thought until Mama declared, "Your grandfather's coming. You'll have to show him the theater sometime."

And then on top of that, "Meet your grandfather at the metro. He'll never find his way on his own."

All the time Mama and Papa have been working in the theater, my grandfather has never once visited them at work. I've taken my classmates to the theater, and Sashok's friends from the country have come to performances and backstage afterward, but my grandfather has never once come. A long time ago he got mad at Mama for going to drama school. And marrying an actor, on top of everything. So mad that he and Mama didn't talk at all for three years. Only after I was born did they make up.

"Couldn't you have chosen a normal profession?"

My grandfather. thinks there are normal professions and ragamuffin professions. Mama should have been a bookkeeper, he thinks, or a dentist, or a lawyer, or at the very worst a teacher. But definitely not an actress.

I don't think there's anything ragamuffin about the theater. One day I'm going to be an actor, like Sam. Or a puppet master, like Lyolik.

Of course, Mama's told me stories about how poor she and Papa were when I was little, that sometimes they didn't have enough money to buy even a spool of thread. She would borrow some from the neighbor — "to sew your little pants." But I don't remember any of that. All I remember is the smell of wood shavings in Lyolik's workshop and the thrill of the puppets coming to life again every evening.

The metro is closer to the theater's public entrance, but I never use that entrance. It's for the audience, the uninitiated. We have an actor's entrance. It's better to go all the way around the theater building than to destroy all the theater magic by walking across the lobby, down the marble staircases, past the cloakroom, and through the big glass doors, where posters in cases are hung a month in advance.

As you're going toward the actor's entrance, sometimes you remember what Sam says about our theater. He says old buildings are much older than they seem. The creaking floorboards, dusty corners, and dried-up beams in the attic, where no one goes for a hundred years at a stretch, give them completely away.

So do the mousy old patrons, the bricks quietly crumbling to dust in the walls, the antique glass door handles that look like thick, unmelted icicles. Even if old buildings get spruced up, even if people fill in the cracks with fresh mortar and smarten them up with new windows, their age still adds up, like the rings of an old tree. Age conceals millions of secrets.

The secrets of our theater are that it once held the Elokhovsky Electro-Theater, the first movie house, and they showed silent films. Before that, people lived in apartments here. It's funny to imagine a kitchen where Sam's dressing room is, for instance, or Lyolik's workshop as someone's bedroom.

You come out of an inconspicuous door — no windows or carved handles — and the first thing you see is the Elokhovskaya Church, which looks like a birch holiday tree ornament. It always seemed to me that the church's name was a little like a pinecone, prickly and fragrant with resin.

Sam used to tell stories about the church and everything, absolutely everything, around it.

He seems to know everything about every building. Moscow is as familiar to him as the stage set for *Karurman: The Black Forest.*

Moscow has become a stage for Sam to walk across, as lightly as when he comes out of the backstage darkness into the phantasmal footlights. Moscow is not just a city but a theater full of mysteries and magic. Sam and I would walk down our street toward Razgulyay Square and come to a famous mansion with columns, and stand there, bewitched, staring at the mysterious metal rectangle between the second-story windows. I would feel chills run down my back and fight the urge to look around, I was so scared. Scared I might see Bruce, the sorcerer, who under Peter the Great either built a magic clock on the side of the building that he later cursed and covered up, or perhaps walled up his own wife there. We would imagine the invisible clock ticking away somewhere inside, if only we could figure out a way to put our ear to the wall up there, and think about how, as the legend goes, the plaque would turn red before times of bloodshed.

Meeting my grandfather at the metro is a completely different thing. It just means jumping over the puddles and the shiny black streetcar rails and waiting for the station entrance to appear with its stern marble columns. No magic at all. My grandfather would be standing by the columns wearing an expensive coat and a black hat.

"Well, now, they only send you out for death," my grandfather mutters, and he takes a deep breath of the cold autumn air through his chiseled nostrils and wiggles his brushy, but neatly trimmed, gray-streaked mustache.

When I'm next to him, I always feel like something's wrong with me. That I'm worse than I really am. That I don't have what it takes to be good in his eyes. My grandfather makes me ashamed of myself — and ashamed of everything I love, too. Like it or not, that's what happens when my grandfather is next to me.

"We have to make a real man of you," he was always saying when I was little. What a "real man" was, exactly, I didn't know, but I knew I didn't want to be one if a real man was anything like my grandfather. "You're raising a sissy," my grandfather would say angrily if my mother gave me a hug.

Once, when they'd left me with him for an evening performance, he said, "Today we're going to watch a movie. A very good movie."

Naturally I wasn't expecting there to be a catch. At first I didn't understand anything I saw. I thought my grandfather had just turned on some movie for grown-ups. But then there was a dark street on the screen and strange people. They were beating someone about the head and back and knocking him to the ground.

A wave of fear washed over me and my stomach felt weird. I covered my eyes so I wouldn't see and waited it out.

But it was still very scary because the guy they were beating kept shouting, so you could tell the kind of thrashing he was getting.

My grandfather suddenly rushed toward me and put his tough hands over mine and jerked them down.

"Look, look," Grandfather snarled, and he held my hands so I couldn't cover my face. "Look! You're no sissy!"

I was so horrified I didn't know where to look, where to turn so I wouldn't see the face on the screen turning into red mush. Then I remembered I could just close my eyes — which I did — and I sat there, crying with closed eyes. My eyelids got all puffy and very, very big, and my mouth was twisted up from all the crying, but I just couldn't stop.

Then my grandfather got scared and ran with me into the kitchen for water, but even there, where I could no longer watch, someone kept crying out in pain, and my insides kept feeling squeezed, and I burst out in convulsive hiccupping, until my grandfather realized he should turn off the television.

I cried all evening until Mama came and took me home. She never left me with my grandfather again — and I was very glad of that. Because I like staying at the theater much more. Sam helps me with my homework, Mama Carlo gives me tea, and Lyolik teaches me to sculpt mouse heads from modeling clay and cook glue for papier-mâché, and to me it seems that this is real life, comfortable and understandable.

With Sam or Lyolik you can just be quiet — and that's fine. But if I'm quiet walking down the street from the metro next to my grandfather, it feels as if I'm doing something wrong. You have to say something — something he wants to hear. But I have no idea what he wants to hear because I don't talk to him often enough. That's why I rattle on about how it rained today and Mama's very glad about him coming to her premiere. My grandfather is quiet and his silence is totally impossible to decipher. I can't figure out whether he's satisfied with me or not.

Showing my grandfather around the theater is like being punished. While Mama and Papa are dancing onstage, I'm walking next to my silent grandfather and picturing my parents and Sam working in the black theater. I picture the velvet backdrop the color of night, the actors dressed in black body stockings, their faces covered with netting. Only by their characteristic movements can you tell that this is Mama, this is Papa, and this is Sam. And then — then a miracle happens. When flowers suddenly appear out of the dark emptiness, they blossom one after the other — violet, blue, and ghoulish red — and then disappear just as quickly, only to blossom again a second later, their petals trembling, at the other end of the stage.

It's so interesting to try to guess where my parents are standing at that moment and which flower they are manipulating.

"So," my grandfather says, coming to a halt in the empty foyer — the audience has all taken their seats — in front of photographs of the actors, and looking at Mama in black and white, smiling, beautiful, like a famous movie star.

"So," my grandfather says, looking over the shoulder of Lyolik, who's carving an anonymous hand, a hand that is no one's yet, out of wood.

"So," my grandfather says, squinting to examine the puppets hanging on the special wooden stand by the stage, their heads hanging lifelessly on the crossbar.

His "so" makes everything seem foolish.

Usually it's only outside the theater that I feel I'm not how non-theater people would like me to be. But next to my grandfather, everything about the theater immediately becomes totally ridiculous and frivolous. For a second you see everything through his eyes. Nothing marvelous, just a very old building and strange people who think they're actors. Who think they're special.

Then my grandfather says, "Queer."

After the show, everyone sets the tables in the theater's snack bar, and it's noisy, merry, and a little tense, and Uncle Kolya — whom we also call Kalinkin or Father Gapon because of his thick beard and the cross around his neck, and also his ability to start arguments — is shouting hoarsely to someone, while Aunt Sveta — who is small and has a long braid that makes her look like a little girl from behind and who always plays girls — is setting out the plates, and Papa is walking between the tables. I keep thinking about what my grandfather said. Thinking and thinking.

What did I expect? What else could he have said? How can he like Sam just because I say he's my good friend? How can I expect my grandfather to smell the theater smell, feel the theater magic, and love it the way I do?

And I answer myself: I can't. I just hadn't thought about it.

I never know what to say when someone calls Sam a queer. If it's a stranger, then I can just turn and leave. But what am I supposed to do with my own grandfather?

I think about this so long my head starts to hurt and I barely hear anything. I barely hear everyone giving toasts, or Lyolik and Mama Carlo arriving, or Sashok darting around the table near me, or her whispering something in my ear about the new puppet master, whom she refers to by the childish nickname Filka instead of Filipp, out of spite.

I suddenly realize I've slept through it all when I see Olezhek holding his glass of champagne very pretentiously and looking at Lyolik. Everyone else is looking at Lyolik too.

"We are very grateful for everything you've done for our theater, Leonid Arkadievich," Olezhek says with feeling. "You and your work — it will remain forever inside the walls of our temple of art."

Sashok starts fidgeting beside me.

"You have earned a dignified old age and a rest," Olezhek continues. "At last we can give you a proper send-off into retirement. A young replacement has arrived, a sapling, basically, and now there is someone to take your place with honor." He nods in Filipp's direction. "To your retirement, Leonid Arkadievich. We wish you a wonderful rest!"

Lyolik sits there looking as if he's suddenly turned into one of his own puppets. Mama Carlo, motionless, stares at Olezhek.

And then I see Sashok's face and get scared she's going to sink her nails into Olezhek's face. Or Filipp's.

"Good thing he's leaving soon," Grandfather says when I show him where the bathroom is. Who's "he"? I don't get it.

"Oh, that Sam of yours. That faggot of yours. Good thing he's leaving soon. The further children can be kept away from those perversions, the better."

"But you're old and you're going to die soon, right?" Sashok asks insolently and loudly — where she's popped up from I have no idea — and stares at my grandfather without blinking.

Once, at a celebration for some premiere, we were running around among the guests and the critics, and all those important people were eating sandwiches and drinking champagne, when suddenly we heard some fat lady critic speaking heatedly to someone else about Sam, who played the lead in the show: "He's gay, but he's a very good actor, as you can see!" Sashok stopped dead in her tracks, stared right into the lady's eyes — when Sashok looks like that, everyone purses their lips and looks away — and said, "Oh, lady! You forgot to shave your mustache. Oh, no!"

I don't know who I'm more ashamed of now: my grandfather; Sashok, who's just been rude again; or myself, because I didn't do anything to stand up for Sam.

"Why don't you come up with something new for a change?" I growl at Sashok and elbow her in the side. At that moment I'm angry at everyone — Sashok, myself, my grandfather, Olezhek, Filka, and even Lyolik. Terribly and hopelessly angry.

Where had Sashok even come from? I recall they haven't actually been introduced yet.

"Grandfather, this is Sashok." I still think I can fix things. It makes Mama happy when I introduce everyone like a human being, and this is her premiere, after all.

"Sashok?" Grandfather raises his eyebrows. "Meaning, Alexandra?"

"Meaning, Sashok," she emphasizes.

"That's a boy's name, not a girl's." My grandfather chuckles. "Do you play with boys' toys too?"

"I'm Sashok because I like being Sashok." Sashok speaks challengingly and raises her voice. "And it doesn't matter, boy or girl."

I start getting nervous. If Sashok gets wound up, there will definitely be trouble.

My grandfather doesn't like people speaking disrespectfully to him.

"I understand, Alexandra," and my grandfather smiles benevolently. Sometimes he looks an awful lot like a nobleman with the whole world at his service.

My grandfather nods haughtily, turns away, and heads for the bathroom. The back of his head says, "They're just silly children, not worth wasting my time."

Sashok turns green. Then white. Her lips are blue. And my palms start sweating.

"Hey, you!"

She grabs my grandfather by the sleeve and pulls as hard as she can — so that you can just barely hear the sleeve rip. My grandfather looks around in astonishment. But Sashok answers him in a muffled yet very distinct voice, "You! You can call your great-grandmother Alexandra, but not me. Is that clear?"

My grandfather leaves the premiere party before everyone else.

"Sodom and Gomorrah," he says, as if he's now finally clear about me, Mama, and Papa. He gives his brushy mustache a tug, picks his hat up off the table, and, bowing his head slightly as if giving his regards to friends, puts it on.

"Grisha will walk you to the metro," Mama begins timidly.

But my grandfather sneers.

"No, thank you; you've already seen me off. I'll find my own way." And he leaves.

"Sodom and Gomorrah," his back repeats.

"Sodom and Gomorrah."

IV

First Snow

THE theater's dark on Mondays. The theater's day off.
There are gray and brittle, lightly frozen autumn leaves,
crumpled, as if an invisible giant had held them in his hand
and thrown them away. There are iced-over puddles by the
door. There's air that smells of imminent snowfalls and is as
crisp as the first snowflakes.

I love the first snow of the year, but it always comes late.
Life is never the way you wish it was.

And there's school on Mondays.

There's school every day, of course, but only on Mondays

is it all-powerful, and there's no getting out of it. Because there's no theater in the evening.

And since there's no getting out of it, the school day drags on endlessly and turns into tough rubber that sticks and winds around everything so that no one can breathe.

"Listen, Grishka," Anton says. "Listen, you look really strange."

"Shtrange-shtrange" — I almost sing it in a stupid voice, and I make a face. I know that right now I look like one of those figurines that jerks its head around; I think the figurine's face is rubber too, so you can smoosh it and make it into anything you want.

"Shtra-a-ange," I say in my best bass voice, like the gym teacher.

"Yes, yes, yes, shtr-a-a-ange," I answer myself in the squeaky voice of the chemistry teacher, who sounds like she's thirteen, not forty.

Anton laughs.

Inside I hate myself, and I'm ashamed of making faces and of my cowardice.

Because inside I bravely tell him, "Listen, Tokha. You're the strange one. I'm just the same as I've always been."

At least, I'm just the same as I was when we were kids and ran away from everyone, went up to the very top floor of the school, and looked down on Moscow. It was fun and awful at the same time. The city lay below, and the transparent air seemed solid, as if you could step on it and slide down.

Remember how we snuck into that old, half-destroyed building past the park and imagined that we were musketeers sitting in ambush, and if they attacked us, we would die for each other?

Everything was simple before. I was just me before. Now that's not enough, for some reason. You have to give as good as you get and look strong. You have to brag that you go to the gym. Or that some girl kissed you. You have to be like everyone else — not just yourself. Because you always feel different. And it's bad and shameful to be different.

That's what I want to tell him.

Instead, I turn into the Jester. And my face becomes the puppet's face.

"A puppet never just talks," Sam once told me. "A puppet never has just words. It speaks and moves simultaneously. There are word-gestures and word-movements, but never just words."

That's why I make faces, and each face is a word. A word Anton can't understand.

The last time he came up to me — everyone else came up to me. At first I didn't understand what they were after. Only later did I understand.

"Come on, Grishka, kiss Katya!" Anton jeered through clenched teeth, and everyone laughed like horses, as if he'd made a good joke.

Katya has big bovine eyes under puffy eyelids, as if she'd just been crying, a heavy gaze, and a big bosom. Katya looked at me as if I'd made her a promise I hadn't kept. Anton gave Katya a light shove, and she nearly fell on top of me — and very close up I could see her thick eyelashes and a birthmark somewhere almost at her temple, and her hair smelled like shampoo but also a little bit like the puppies that ran around the courtyard.

Everyone — I could feel their looks on my skin — stood there gawking at me as if I were an animal in the zoo. Waiting.

I looked at her mouth, which seemed very close — it smelled of something sickly sweet and weird — and I felt a little queasy, whether from the smell or the fact that everyone was staring at us and waiting.

I just stood in front of Katya and stared at the floor so I wouldn't have to look into her cow eyes and see her right eyelid twitching. I examined the tips of my sneakers and listened to her breathe — I could even feel her breath on my face. She didn't say anything either, but then she gave my shoulder a shove — hard, rough, not the way little girls shove — softly breathed out "jerk," turned around, and walked off.

"You're the jerks," I threw out at Anton.

But today the Jester in me is trying to get in good with him, as if the whole thing were my fault. As if I ought to have kissed Katya — even though I couldn't.

The Jester makes fun of Anton and disdains him. He laughs to keep from crying.

He makes faces so he doesn't seem serious, no matter what.

The gym locker room smells of sweat and dirty jerseys. After a show at the theater, everyone rushes to the dressing rooms, wet too, of course, and changes clothes, tossing their shirts and pants on the old leather couches, but the theater also smells of glue, makeup, and perfume, the hot air from the lamps over the dressing tables, and hairspray. I love the smell of the dressing rooms after a show, and I hate the school locker room.

That's why I change fast, to get out of there as soon as possible. But now Anton and I are the last ones left.

At first I don't understand why he's looking at me so strangely or why he suddenly turns away, as if he is shy in front of me.

"What's wrong with you? Lost your marbles?"

"Well, don't take this the wrong way. But, I don't know — what if you really are gay? That's what people say. It's popular with you theater people."

"People say?" I feel as if I've run out of air and have nowhere to get it to take a breath. "Who says?"

"Well, people."

And Anton looks away. I look away too. I can't look him in the eye — whether out of embarrassment, or because my face is all hot and red, or out of fear.

He just mumbles, "You've gotten so strange — weird, kind of. Not like us."

Monday is loneliness, that's for sure. If every day was a Monday, what then?

Even the saddest Tuesdays are better than cheerful Mondays.

Tuesday is Lyolik's last day in the theater. I keep thinking Olezhek is going to change his mind at any moment and everything will stay the way it was.

"Grisha, take the sketches to the artists," Mama Carlo says. Lyolik looks over his glasses as I take the thick folder with the time-ragged edges. He watches and smooths out a piece of glue-soaked newspaper that he's sculpted on a clay mold. One day it will be a big-mouthed mask with enormous eyes.

Both Mama Carlo and Lyolik — if you looked at them, you'd never say that after tonight's show he's going to gather up his things and go home. Retire — for good. Oh, he might come by sometimes, but as a visitor, not the master.

Even Filipp, who's sitting next to Lyolik like an apprentice, watching him work — "learning" — even he looks as if they're going to keep sitting that way tomorrow, and the day after tomorrow, and for all eternity. As if Lyolik isn't going anywhere.

Only the two old suitcases on the floor by the radiator give it all away. Two old suitcases heaped with patterns, drawings, and controllers, a few shabby old puppet heads, and some wires: That's all Lyolik is taking with him.

This time, I don't think it would help even if I ran through the whole theater at breakneck speed. To see Aunt Tanya, the wardrobe mistress, shouldering a huge pile of dresses with lace frills and a uniform, and Vanya, the light tech, carrying a heavy spotlight.

And to hear Boyakin, the actor who looks like a hero from a folktale with his curly hair, exhaling smoke in the smoking lounge, say about Sam, "Good thing it's soon. Finally some decent roles will open up."

And to stumble on the marble stairs and drop the file and bruise my knee badly.

The sketches go flying, fluttering down and off to the side like white birds, and fly into the corners, but Sashok catches them, as if they're tame birds. As if she's always waiting around here to leap out when you least expect her. Usually I don't care, but when you're lying there like an idiot on the stairs and your knee is stinging — it can make you crazy.

"Are you following me or something?"

"Are you some kind of fool? I'm helping you. Say 'thank you' and don't be a pig!"

"Anyway, you're a pig," she sums up when we leave the artists' garret where you can see the park and bookstore out the narrow window and the Elokhovskaya Church in the distance.

Everyone is standing by the little door to the shortcut to the lobby and the coatroom. You duck your head and go down a secret passage, and from there it's a couple of steps to Olezhek's office. Kalinkin-Father Gapon, Aunt Sveta, Mama and Papa, Boyakin, Sashok's papa, and everyone else.

And Sam.

"You just have to go and make it clear!" Sam is saying. "Just ask! What's it worth?"

"*You* go make it clear," Father Gapon says in his bass voice. "*You* go ask."

"It's easy for you to be brave," Boyakin jeers. "It doesn't cost you anything, naturally. You're hightailing it out of here soon. But we have to get along with him" — and he nods in the direction of Olezhek's office.

Sam purses his lips, turns, and pushes the low door. He bends over and strides into the secret passage. And all of them — Father Gapon; Boyakin; Aunt Sveta; Vinnik the actress; and Timokhin, who's as plump as a roll; every last one of them — stand there and watch him go.

Then Mama steps into the passage. And Papa. And Sashok's papa. And no one else.

The door springs shut softly as it runs into the foam that covers the doorjamb.

"Step on it!" Sashok whispers in my ear. And we step on it.

As though if we run fast enough, Lyolik will stay at the theater.

The door to Olezhek's office is open. We can see Olezhek standing behind his desk, as if fending off Sam and Mama and Papa and Sashok's papa.

"There's nothing I can do, kid. Nothing," he says almost pathetically. "I'm between a rock and a hard place, understand?"

Kolokolchikov raises a short eyebrow, and his eyes go flat.

"We're all in the same boat. Kid, you have to understand, I got a request from there" — and he nods at the ceiling, as if someone lives there — "to give his son a job. What can I do?"

He spreads his arms helplessly.

"Why can't there be two puppet masters? Can't you spare the cash?" Sam is seething. "Where are you going to find another master like Lyolik? Filipp won't be able to cope alone."

"It's the money. There is none, my dear man. You're expensive, my dear Sam! Where am I supposed to get money for two wages?" Kolokolchikov's voice becomes affectionate, as if he's talking to a wayward child.

"He's lying," Sashok whispers to me. "He's definitely lying. Lying eyes!"

"Isn't it time for you to get changed and made up, my friends?" Kolokolchikov glances at the clock. "Time waits for no man."

And he comes out from behind his desk to close the door after his visitors.

"Well, at least we tried," Papa says, sighing, when they find themselves in the lobby.

One-two-three, one-two-three: The lights are being switched on onstage and in the theater, the lights are being switched on on the Christmas tree, and snow is starting to fall. Snow to the rhythm of the "Waltz of the Snowflakes." It's tossed up and seems to sweep across the stage; it falls and falls on the heads of the quiet audience; and somewhere an invisible chorus is singing delicately. And even if it is just light, even if it is Maika somewhere in the balcony doing her magic to make it look like real snow onstage and in the audience, still this snowstorm is just like real life. Even if the person in the black cape and top hat on the proscenium is Papa, even if somewhere back there Sam is getting ready for his entrance. Still, this snow is the real thing — and the fairy tale is the real thing too. Even if there, outside, it's still fall and we still have to wait for snow.

In the theater, nothing's like real life. If you want something badly enough, it has to happen.

While the show is going on, I help Lyolik pack his suitcases. I asked to help; after all, when you're doing something, it's not as sad.

For the time being you don't have to think about what it'll be like to come to the workshops and find only Filipp and Mama Carlo, and no Lyolik. About whether the Candy Puppet Show will open again if Lyolik doesn't come to the theater anymore. Will Lyolik make his own puppets at home? What is he going to do there?

When you think about how people get decommissioned — because it really is being decommissioned — it's like a puppet getting decommissioned from an old show. They decommission you if you're old, like Lyolik, or if you're not like everyone else, if you're someone like Sam.

We pack the last drawings and old notebooks, which look like they're a hundred years old, into the suitcase. We pack old photographs of bearded marionettes with strange, enormous eyes and seams on their jaws.

"Puppets from Brno," Lyolik says. "Made from nineteenth-century drawings. At one time they put on shows in the terrible dungeons where emperors once held criminals. The audience sat right on the floor, and the lighting was like in olden times — just candles."

◆

Lyolik isn't saying good-bye to anyone. "I can't stand good-byes," he says. "It's all such foolishness." We leave by the actors' entrance. Sam carries Lyolik's frayed suitcases, and

Sashok lugs a small box with pieces of wood. Lyolik puts on a good face and pretends all this is nothing — leaving the theater he only wanted to leave carried out feet first.

"Good luck, Leonid Arkadievich," Albert Ilich, the janitor, says, tearing himself away from the television for a second. "Good luck" — Lyolik nods, as if he were just going out for half an hour, to the store.

We go out, and it feels as if we've landed in another world and another time.

In the light of the streetlamp, the sky and the black street flash, spin, and waltz to invisible music.

The Elokhovskaya Church is a somber painting with a ripple running across it, a snow ripple.

And an invisible chorus seems to be singing somewhere, like in the show.

"It's a little early." Sam sighs.

"Not at all," Lyolik says.

It's just the first snow falling. Without a sound, and thick.

It's snowing.

It covers the grass, which isn't completely dried out yet or really frozen, and the roofs of cars, and Sashok's nose — where it melts because Sashok is so hot. The black paths turn white, as if someone has decided to paint them in one fell swoop, and the fine sleet turns to fluffy flakes and falls and falls, covering everything with a thick milky fog, crunching like lemon wafers, and smelling of ice.

The first snow.

It's come early — on purpose, to see Lyolik off.

V

An Extended Intermission

I'm the king's favorite jester,
Though I'm often called a fool.
My specialty is laughter,
But I'm smarter than a jewel.
Smarter than the prince I am,
Smarter than the King of Siam!
His cap has no bell to ring in your ear,
Not a single jingle your heart to cheer!
— from The Glass Slipper, *by Tamara Gabbe*

THE music is playing softly and the Jester is walking across the stage. Sam — you'd never recognize him in his body stocking and pointy-toed shoes and his jester's cap, and his eyes seem huge in makeup — speaks as if he were singing.

Scraps of cloth flash by — cornflower blue, gooseberry purple, apple red.

Sam hasn't been Sam for a long time; his face has melded into the Jester's — and there are two jesters onstage and not a single Sam. His face isn't still for a minute, and his nose and eyebrows have a life of their own as they form a moving mask — and the way Sam raises his eyebrows, everyone in the very last row can see every movement of his face, the Jester's face.

First he walks across the stage, practically dancing, then he flies lightly up, as if he weighs less than a gram, and he points his toe as if this were the most natural thing in life — to fly over the earth and point your toe. He lands on one knee, playfully, and you believe it really is that easy, then he flies across the stage like a pinwheel, and then gives a hop and does handsprings backward, weightless and flexible.

When he picks up a puppet, you forget right away that there was just a person there.

Sam's hands become one with the crossbar; they grow into it; they extend the marionette's string-sinews; they turn into a pendulum as the Jester comes to life. As if Sam has lent him his whole self for the performance.

The Jester winks and looks around with clever eyes, is amazed and laughs and becomes so grand, you'd think there were no other roles or puppets in the show.

◆

The light cannons fire incredible colors, and the spotlights are aimed at the stage. The light symphony is insane: Light splashes as if the stage itself has turned into a colorful jester's costume.

I'm sitting in the balcony near Maika's light booth and holding my breath as I watch the stage — trying not to miss a single one of Sam's movements.

I don't think Sam has ever acted this well.

I think, *The Glass Slipper* is going away and taking everyone with it: the Jester puppet; Sam, who plays him best of all; and Lyolik, who made all the puppets for the show.

I've already found an old gym bag in the closet and brought it to the theater. When they give me the Jester, I'll hide him there, so Sashok won't notice. And then I'll give him to her for her birthday.

If you could put people in a bag, I'd have hidden Sam there, to keep him from leaving. To keep him close always.

Before the show, I hung around his dressing room like a homeless mutt.

I used to hang around him all the time when he was getting ready for a show. I just couldn't leave for a minute. But then he started sending me out when he was changing.

After I suddenly froze, looking at him once.

It seems like only yesterday that Sam would stay with me when my parents did a show out of town, instead of the grandmother I didn't have. Dear Sam, who patiently taught me spelling tricks at the makeup table.

Suddenly I saw him in a completely different light.

Sam caught my look — as if we were fencing in a show and he'd nimbly deflected my sword upward.

He caught my look and his eyes turned dark; his eyes looked at me with surprise and suspicion. As if some stranger had suddenly caught him undressed.

"On your way, Grisha. Go play," he said, and he lightly turned me toward the door and gave me a little push, as if he were afraid I wouldn't go.

"Why? You always let me be here when you're changing!"

"And now I'm not. No reason. Go on, then, go on. Step lively!"

Since then, I've always waited for him by his dressing room.

I've been lonely. Sashok is never here, after all. She's made herself scarce.

Sashok declared war on Filipp. Right after Lyolik left.

"No mercy," is how she puts it.

"Filka," she taunts whenever she sees him, and turning away, she twists her bluish lips.

She drips paint on his chair, sprinkles nails in his glue, and hides the artists' drawings and sketches where Filipp won't find them. But the worst thing — cutting the puppets' straps somewhere on top, at the crossbar — that, she would not do.

Sometimes Filipp finds her in the workshop, and then she bolts.

"Stupid kid!" he hollers after her, and runs out of the workshop.

"Pimple! Butthead! Master-who's-not!" Sashok's voice breaks as she runs out of his reach.

"Stop it!" Olezhek gets mad from time to time. "I'm sick of it. If you keep this up, kid" — he's talking to Sashok — "I'll ban you from the theater. Understand, kid?"

Sashok stubbornly purses her lips, and her eyes become just like a wolf's, and she glowers at Olezhek.

The next evening it happens all over again. Because everyone knows Olezhek can't ban Sashok or fire the shouting Filipp.

"I'm going to make his life a misery," Sashok says vengefully. "He'll be the one wanting to leave. You'll see — and soon!"

"Filka's a jerk!" she shouts at him from the doorway. Provided Mama Carlo isn't in the workshop — because once she heard Sashok say, "Filka's a jerk," and she chewed her out: "Now, you may be able to take that tone at home. But not around me!"

Sashok wages her war, but Filka still isn't quitting. She sits down on the black painted stairs leading from the workshops to the stage and the dressing rooms and stubbornly bows her head, as if she wants to butt through all the walls on earth.

"Are you going to help me, or what?" she asks, and she seems close to tears. But she only seems like that — Sashok isn't likely to cry.

"Fool." She gets mad when I bring her glue instead of paint. "I can't trust you to do anything."

I understand that all this is wrong somehow, but I can't explain why even to myself. Sometimes I feel sorry for Filipp, but then I remember that it's his fault they made Lyolik retire, and anger wells up inside me.

I also think I'm a coward and a wimp and can't make up my mind to do anything.

It's Sashok who just knows that she has to get back at Filipp, and she'll stop at nothing, like a small bulldozer.

The theater isn't the old theater anymore.

It's like a tour bus for out-of-town shows.

I stop by the workshops, see Filipp, and realize I stopped by to see Lyolik, who isn't sitting in his usual spot anymore — the high chair where he could see the people out the window and the actors in the hallway.

Only Filipp is sitting at the master's table and chiseling something out of wood — his skinny shoulder blades bobbing up and down under his T-shirt, and the colorful dragon tattoo on his chicken wing wiggling its mustache. Filipp glances briefly at me, lifts a corner of his mouth as if uncertain, and tugs his goatee. His earring sparkles in the lamplight.

It feels colder than usual in the workshops.

It's as if some strange intermission has started and just can't end.

And it's dragging on and on — indefinitely.

It should be over already — so that Lyolik will return, and Sam will rehearse a new part, and the awful feeling that everything is changing will go away.

Sam and I have gone to see Lyolik at home a few times. He opens the door for us, nods briefly, as if he isn't happy to see us, and wanders deep inside the inexplicably dark apartment where he lives with Mama Carlo.

"When she comes home from work, she'll wash them" — he gestures in the direction of the dirty cups and saucers on the table and turns toward the window, where you can see the river, the streams of cars, and the illuminated sharp-winged eagles on the tower of the Kiev Train Station.

They're giving him a place at the Home for Veterans of the Stage soon, Lyolik says. "Very, very soon. I'll be hearing soon."

"Why the Home? Why the Home?" I feel like shouting. But instead I watch how Sam talks with Lyolik, as if he's a wayward child.

Unembarrassed, he takes Lyolik's wrinkled hand and strokes it. He nearly gets down on his knees, pleading.

"Listen, why do you need that? Your sister's here. Your home's here."

"I don't want to be a burden to anyone. If I'm not needed in the theater, it's better that I be in the Home. My sister is at work day in and day out — at least there are people there."

I feel like shouting to Lyolik, "Think about what your Efimovich said! You're decommissioning yourself!" But I hold my tongue.

Once, I asked him to help me to make a puppet. I thought that would cheer him up. But he just shook his head. "No. I won't. I've already made all my puppets. That's enough."

◆

Today we are accompanying Lyolik to the Home for Veterans of the Stage.

On our way to his house, I sit in the front seat next to Sam and am selfishly happy that there is a lot of traffic and I can be with Sam like this for a long time.

"Don't you mind that you're leaving and your parents are staying here?" I've wanted to ask Sam about that for a long time. I know they barely see one another.

Once I happened to hear Sam talking to Lyolik: "When my father found out, he shouted at first. I remember his face to this day. Then he said, 'Don't sit at the same table with us.' Then he told me to take my plate, cup, fork, and knife and wash them myself, 'so I wouldn't infect everyone.' Then he completely pretended I didn't exist. And then I left home.

"My mama? She doesn't want to upset my father. She probably has no use for me. The way I am."

At the time I thought I'd overheard — not that I'd been trying to — something completely forbidden, something I shouldn't know. I've never brought it up, and Sam's never told me anything about his parents.

Sam is silent for a long, long time. He looks straight ahead, tensely, though we're stopped at a light and not moving. His olive-skinned hands are perfectly still, resting on the steering wheel as if they're made of stone, and only his pointer finger taps a rhythm, audible to Sam alone, very, very lightly on the dark blue matte cover.

"They don't have a son. That's how they talk," he says suddenly. "But Lyolik, he's different. I don't know how I can leave him here now."

In the early November twilight, Lyolik's building looks like a big shark's tooth, but in fact it's shaped like a horseshoe. Cars rush by, purple-tinged windows are reflected in the Moscow River, and the snow in Lyolik's courtyard is dark and boring. We wait in the car by the front door, and I don't recognize Lyolik right away. He seems very small now, dried out, sort of. "Well, shall we go?" he asks in a lackluster voice. He isn't joking the way he used to or smiling at Sam.

Going to the Home is completely different this time.

The streets seem darker, except that in the lot near the Home where Sam parks his car, the newly fallen snow makes it lighter. The snow crunches and creaks underfoot, as if we are stepping over candy wrappers, and like the last time, the twilight smells sweet and sharp from wood smoke, and the violet paths run off into the woods.

The Home looks dark and empty. Efimovich isn't even there. "He's in the hospital," Lyolik says drily, and he disappears behind the door marked ADMINISTRATION.

"I've got another month to wait," he says with a sigh later, as he gets into the car.

"Listen, Lyolik," Sam says.

"Don't start," Lyolik says sullenly, so that Sam can only be quiet.

We walk Lyolik to his apartment, and as we're going back downstairs to the courtyard, I suddenly see Sam's eyes flashing.

"What's wrong, Sam?"

Onstage, Sam can cry at will. With a wave of a magic wand. Ever since I was a kid, I've watched his eyes suddenly fill with tears, his face instantly turn to stone, and a tear trace a line through his makeup. And it's always a miracle, inexplicable and a little frightening.

"How do you do that, Sam?" I used to ask.

"I don't." He shrugged. "It just seems to happen."

But only once have I ever seen Sam cry offstage.

That was a long time ago. He and a friend were attacked on the street, not far from the theater.

"He was just holding my hand."

Covered in bruises and scratches, Sam went to the workshop to see Mama Carlo and Lyolik.

I was proud of him, because there were three of them and he was alone. And they ran away first. Someone with muscles like Sam's — of course he'd win, I believed. Sashok clicked her tongue in admiration.

But Sam suddenly dropped his head in his hands — so no one would see his eyes — and started weeping. I only guessed he was weeping because his shoulders were quaking.

Mama Carlo calmly dipped a cotton swab in a vial of iodine and drew a comic book strongman on Sam's shoulders.

Sashok ran around him and could only ask, "So what happened, Sam? What's the matter? You beat them — you beat them, didn't you? What's the matter, Sam?"

"I'm a pig and a coward," he suddenly said angrily. "Just a pig."

But now he looks at me as if I am his age, as if I can understand absolutely everything.

"I decommissioned myself when I decided to leave. Understand? They see you off way before you actually leave. Everyone gets used to the idea of you not being there, and they act as if you're not you anymore. You can't keep pretending — it doesn't work.

"I'm going where other people have made sure I won't get called a homo or get beaten in an entryway. Other people — not me. Because I'm a coward. But I don't know how I can go on here. I just don't know. I can't just go abandon Lyolik. And I can't not leave. My resignation letter's been signed. They've brought in others to take my parts. There's a buyer coming tomorrow to look at the apartment. And that's that."

He falls silent. "That's all of it. Except for the leaving."

Suddenly, into the frosty silence Sam says angrily, "They'd probably remember him only if all the puppets broke at the same time."

And at that moment it seems to me as if somewhere in the world a light has been switched on, and all at once I can see everything that has been hiding in the dark corners.

If. All. The puppets. Broke. At the same time.

VI

PUPPETS ALIVE

"IN life, as onstage, if you do nothing, then nothing happens," Sam likes to say.

"You're nuts, Grisha." Sashok doesn't believe me at first. "Totally nuts," she repeats, concentrating on tapping the spot between her thumb and pointer finger.

She's picked up this gesture recently, and it drives me impossibly crazy. "It's a kind of treatment," Sashok explains, as if her stupid tapping could cure her heart.

We're sitting on the iron stairs in the puppet room. Sashok calls the stairs the "roost." Because they're narrow, iron, and steep, but on top, like a metal nest, there's a landing for props.

Right above our heads, on the shelves, are papier-mâché apples, pretzel braids that, if you look closely, are actually wound gauze bandages under the paint, wooden wagon wheels, and enormous spoons.

Below are the partitions hung with puppets and masks. You can make out the tops of the kings' and queens' heads, and their glued-on wigs, and the sharp noses with their skillfully chiseled nostrils — as if they're alive. Lyolik's puppets always come out totally alive.

Sashok and I like to climb up high and sit there, like the captains of the puppet ship, all alone among them.

"I'm so sick of them! All of them!" Sashok says angrily just as we sit down. She mimics, *"Do you have a boyfriend? Who do you like?* I feel like saying something nasty, just for spite."

I nod. It's true, I'm sick of some grown-ups.

"Do you have a girlfriend?"

As if the sky will fall on my head if I don't. As if I'll grow donkey ears if I don't.

Even at the theater, Aunt Sveta or, say, the actress Vinnik, will come up and say, "Which girls do you like in school?"

Why don't they ask what I'm reading, for instance?

I try to make myself scarce. I pretend I'm in a big hurry. I hate those stupid conversations.

"What do you tell them?" I ask Sashok. She shrugs.

" 'Well,' I say, 'you'll faint; I fell in love with Shakespeare a few days ago.' Then they laugh. I tell others, the stupider ones, Gabanek. Gabanek, of course, makes a bigger impression. At least he's a foreigner, they think."

What would you do without Gabanek, Sashok? I think. What would you do without the fat-cheeked dragon-marionette from the Czech fairy tale? What would you and I do without the theater?

"No, you really are nuts," Sashok continues after she hears about the puppets. "Break them all?"

To be honest, I think I'm nuts too. I think about it every day, roll it around on my tongue like a caramel Sam has tossed me: "if-all-the-puppets-broke-at-the-same-time."

After all, then Olezhek would have no choice. He'd have to ask Lyolik to fix them. Only Lyolik knows his puppets well enough to fix them all quickly.

They'll have no other choice, I think. But then I go to the puppet room and pick up the slender hands of the courtiers and hunters, the dressed-up ladies and ethereal fairies, and the velvety paws of the foxes and mice. I look into their puppet eyes — huge or craftily squinting, subtly drawn right down to the specks around the pupils, or simple ones that look like ordinary buttons. And I have no idea how I could break them, even for Lyolik's sake. How could I? Even if that would bring him back and keep him from the charity home forever? How could I break their arms, cut their straps and strings, and then look at their dangling, broken legs in their neat little boots, and their sunken, half-open, dead-seeming eyes?

After all, a puppet is alive — unless you break it.

"You can understand what's inside a puppet, and you can learn how to operate it. But the puppet decides how you're going to work with it. The puppet," Lyolik once said.

"It won't work for you to adapt the puppet to you. You can break it, but you can't force it to be the way you want," Sam repeated.

Sashok sits for a long time staring at the puppets' curls and feathered hats, at their bald spots and straight puppet parts.

She's probably thinking the same thing I am.

"What a mess," she mutters, and jumps down from the roost, spreading her arms in Sam's trademark gesture, as if an invisible and weightless parachute is opening over the ground.

"Fine, then," I tell myself, so that Sashok won't hear or

guess. "Fine, then. I'll do it myself. Alone. For Lyolik I can do it. All the puppets. Even if it's hard."

Sashok walks over to the slender-necked puppet Lyudmila, touches her rod, and straightens her dark green dress, unfolding its seemingly whimsical curl. And it looks as though Lyudmila is reaching her fragile hand out to me.

"Sashok, just don't say a word to anyone later, that it was me. Please, Sashok!" That's what I want to tell her.

Sashok turns around and sighs.

"Well, if you're nuts, then so am I. Nuts." And she busies herself with straightening Lyudmila's dress again.

"Hmm" is all I can get out. And she, of course, has no idea how happy I am.

❖

The theater has woken up and come back to life.

We go missing in the puppet room for days on end.

It's like sitting in a besieged enemy town. Our battlements are the partitions hung with marionettes and Punches, with rod puppets and huge masks.

"We aren't touching the masks," Sashok says sternly. "There aren't very many of them, anyway. They're not important."

We bring our parents' books of drawings and patterns from home, and Sashok traces out with her finger: "Cut over here and over here."

Sometimes we argue.

"What is it with you, you jerk?" Sashok boils up. "You have to cut it from the inside. Then Filka definitely can't repair it — but Lyolik can. I'll bring a good knife. My papa has one," she says.

Sam peeks in — "Want to go to the snack bar?" — but we shake our heads. Later. Later. Though I know there won't be a Sam later.

We tell the curious we're just playing.

We examine the control rods — the puppet spines — the wooden rods hidden inside under the costume, to which the puppet mechanism is attached. I never knew before that they could be so different. That there could be pistol control rods, flexible ones, that there could be such clever joints. That the control rod handles the actor holds the puppet by are as varied as human hands — so they're easy for everyone to work. That the dowels can just be square but some have a convenient hole chiseled out for the thumb.

We examine the lines and hooks and touch the rough dowels so we can understand how they're all secured.

The puppets wink, throw out a little knee, bow their heads, shrug their shoulders, and clap their hands. That's when I think that at the very last moment I won't be able to, I won't be able to cut the sinew-strings on a single puppet. I won't be able to break what Lyolik has done, even if it's to bring him back.

Sashok goes around downcast too. "I won't be able to," she says. And we're silent. Then we go back to examining the drawings and working the marionettes' levers over and over again, like practicing the piano. "If you cut it here and here, then you have to open up the head to repair it. Do you know how hard that is?"

When I picture having to open up a head — on my Jester, for instance — my fingers start to shake and I feel a nasty chill in my stomach. That's when I start saying mentally, "Oh, forgive me, forgive me, but you have to understand. What else can I do?"

I still feel like a criminal, though.

"We have to do it all during the day," Sashok reflects. "Then they'll still have time to find Lyolik and bring him back to the theater. He'll be able to repair the puppets before the evening performance."

First we'll go after the *Nutcracker* puppets, we decide. After all, they're performing it this evening. I mean, if we can't break them all, we'll break the most important ones so they'll have to cancel the performance. Or think of Lyolik.

The theater isn't about to doze off and die after all. It's sighing and sometimes even laughing, and the floor in the hall between the dressing rooms shakes ever so slightly. The theater's iron railings rumble and the costumes rustle. The longest intermission ever seems to be coming to an end.

We're walking from the workshops past the set storage room, and my palms are sweating. I think anyone we run into now must know that Sashok has a small knife in her pocket. And kitchen scissors, to make it easier to cut the straps.

I always like coming close to the puppet room. But today, for the first time, I'm scared. I'm afraid of the puppets. I'm afraid of myself and what I'm planning to do. And even more afraid that at the very last moment I'll turn coward and not do it.

I wonder whether Sashok is thinking the same thing, when we stop at the door to the puppet room and then fling it open.

It feels as if we're just about to jump from high up into a huge snowdrift.

The room is quiet. It's never that quiet in the theater, I think.

Sashok and I stand in this quiet, and she says softly, "I'll bet it's going to start raining right now — right here, under the roof."

And suddenly a crack in the corner breaks the silence. Sashok shudders.

Then there's a crack in another.

Click-clack-click — as if some invisible person is cracking walnuts under the holiday tree.

Click-clack-crrrack.

Louder and louder, as if the whole room has all at once come to life and started knocking, cracking, and breaking, like a walnut shell.

And it seems — but only seems, of course — as if the puppets, every last one of them — Jester, Fairy, Hortensia and Javotta, Nutcracker, Tin Soldier — are smiling at us ever so slightly.

"Grisha!" Sashok whispers. "Look at that!"

She runs over to the Jester, raises his arm — and it hangs lifelessly. Not the way a resting puppet usually does, springy and tensed close to the body, but as if the Jester has suddenly lost all his strings.

As if we really had used Sashok's papa's knife to cut all the marionettes' sinews and broken all their control rods.

"What a mess," Sashok mutters, running from the mice to Losharik, from Lyudmila to Cinderella.

"They're broken! All of them! The puppets! At the same time! Broken!"

We look at each other — and then start to laugh.

Sashok clucks like a bustling hen, and I laugh so hard my stomach hurts. Our fear drains from us with the laughter. We laugh for joy, that we haven't had to, we haven't had to break Lyolik's puppets.

"The puppets are broken!" Sashok shouts, as if she isn't quite right in the head, and choking with laughter, she runs down the hall.

"The puppets are broken!" I repeat after her.

"The puppets are broken," she gurgles for the last time into the fat belly of Timokhin the actor, who she's slammed into near the men's dressing rooms.

"Why are you shouting? What's broken?" Timokhin asks with a puzzled look.

That's when we come to our senses, we're so happy, and I murmur, "There. All the puppets, all of them, are broken, just now" — and I nod toward the puppet room.

"That can't be," Sam says, and he looks at me very, very closely.

I just about drop through the earth, because only then do I realize what he must be thinking about me.

The theater starts murmuring, speaking, tramping, and rustling. It has conversations in different voices, it slams doors, it creaks open window vents, its steps snarl, and it laughs delicately, strumming the iron stairs. The dressing room doors creak and slam, as if they've decided to run a marathon and are rushing endlessly back and forth.

"That's how it always is!" Father Gapon murmurs, and he gathers his beard in his hand. "The lords fight, and the peasants pay the price!"

"Hell's bells! Hell's bells!" Sultanov, a very old actor, repeats indignantly.

"That's all right. The show must go on," Sam says, trying to keep their spirits up.

"What?" Boyakin exclaims. "What? We'll go on as the puppets? Where? Where has anyone seen that?"

"It's time to retire," Vinnik the actress says in her husky voice.

Aunt Sveta silently stirs sugar in her cup so hard it looks as if the spoon is about to smash the cup to pieces. They don't hear the bell at all, they're shouting so loudly.

"It's a madhouse! It's curtains! It's a mess!" Papa exclaims tragically, and he runs out into the corridor to smoke.

"Something like this could only happen in this theater! This one! Mark my word! Theaters are theaters everywhere, but this one is a mess. A mess! I have to get out!" Timokhin hollers. "And go to a decent theater!"

"Has anyone invited you?" Mama gives him a dubious look.

"Well, I mean . . . in principle." Timokhin backs down immediately.

Filipp runs up — and his already short hair seems to be standing on end. Striding into the puppet room, he dashes from one puppet to the next, examines the controllers, and tests the control rods.

"Exactly. Broken," he says through his teeth, and he stares at Sashok.

"What are you looking at? Back off, you old goat," she snarls as usual, but she turns away to escape his eyes.

Olezhek is moving down the hall with his awkward, rolling gait. His legs are rowing nervously, like flippers. His face is stark white, and his eyes have faded even more, to the point of complete transparency.

"Well, how bad is it?" He nods at Filipp and grabs his sleeve.

"What can I say?" Filipp responds sullenly. "All the puppets are broken. Including the ones for today's show."

The clamor and din start back up: "It's a mess!" "In this theater!" "How can we act with dummies?"

"Actors always come last!"

"Who did this?" Olezhek screams, and from behind, you can see his head shaking ever so slightly.

It gets very quiet. No one is shouting anymore. Papa stubs out his cigarette. Even Father Gapon stands there very quietly.

The theater falls very quiet too.

Sam — I can see — is trying his hardest not to look at me.

Olezhek's eyes dart from side to side, as if they'll break at any moment, like on a tired old puppet.

And then they stop on Sashok.

"You?" Olezhek says softly. "Did you do this?" And he adds, "Your parents will have to pay for everything."

"I did it!" I want to say, and even take half a step forward and inhale a full chest of air.

But I'm too late.

Because Filipp blurts out, "Oh, all right. It was me. I broke them."

And everyone stares at Filipp: Sam, Olezhek, Mama and Papa, and Father Gapon.

Sashok's mouth actually falls open. "Crazy!" she whispers admiringly, and I elbow her in the side as hard as I can to get her to pipe down. Olezhek is awful to look at. He turns pale, then red, then some impossible shade of yellow.

"You?" he helplessly asks Filipp. "But why? Why would you?"

"I realized I couldn't cope, Oleg Borisovich," Filipp begins, as if suddenly inspired. "So I got mad. I'm pretty high-strung, Oleg Borisovich. My papa says I'm a psycho."

"Your papa," Kolokolchikov responds very softly.

Of course, there's no way Filipp will be able to repair even half the puppets by the evening's performance.

"Lyolik!" Olezhek's face shines. "I'll call him and he'll help."

"He won't agree," Sam says quickly. "Even if you pay well."

"He won't?" Olezhek repeats, stunned, and his lower lip starts trembling.

"Naturally," Timokhin says bitingly. "You didn't even give him a proper retirement party, Oleg Borisovich!"

Everyone starts clamoring.

"I'll try to convince him" — Sam looks hard into Olezhek's eyes — "but I doubt I'll be able to."

Olezhek grabs his sleeve.

"You'll try? Tell him we're sorry, well, that things worked out the way they did — without a proper retirement party."

Sam gently removes his hand.

"Only nothing's going to happen that simply."

"That simply?" Olezhek seems to understand what Sam is talking about and is trying as hard as he can to delay the moment when he'll have to say it out loud.

"Yes, that simply," Sam repeats harshly. "Now, if you were to give me an order restoring puppet master Leonid Arkadievich's position . . ."

"An order" — and Olezhek heaves a doomed sigh.

"I'm sorry. I completely forget there aren't any extra wages," Sam says sadly.

"Oh, we'll find a wage, we will, kid!" Olezhek goes for it. "Please, Sam, will you speak to him?"

"I'll try," Sam says sternly, and he turns around. And we can see that his eyes are laughing.

"Tell him we're all asking him," Papa sums up. "Every last one of us!"

It's absolutely as if the theater has woken up. It seems to be dancing to jazz music no one else can hear, and I feel like dancing with it, snapping my fingers and hopping around.

Of course, we all tag along to see Lyolik.

"Let's run to the metro!" Sam shouts to us, thrusting the order restoring Lyolik to his post, with Olezhek's hooked signature, into his bag. "Step lively!"

It hasn't started to grow dark yet — and of course there will be time to fix the puppets.

At Baumanskaya Station, I touch the knee of the bronze pilot wearing the warm flight suit so everything will work out and Lyolik will come back to the theater for good.

Sam is smiling privately at something. Sashok and I stand on the train with our noses pressed to the window that says, DO NOT OPEN. Someone has rubbed out a couple of letters to form the illiterate DO NOT PE. Not that it's written for us, of course. We watch spliced cables turning into savage snakes and solitary lamps flickering, and we try to guess the mysterious stations and abandoned tunnels in the velvety, coal-scented darkness.

All of a sudden, I say, probably hoping Sashok won't hear me in the noise and whistling of the train going through the tunnel: "They call me a queer. Because I don't kiss girls."

She moves away, and a puddle of steam melts on the window and slowly dissipates, as if someone has blown it off the glass. She glances at me sideways and mutters something — I think she says, "We'll figure something out" — and presses her forehead back on the glass. Then she presses her hands to the glass too, as if she's closing herself off from everyone. On her palms you can probably see lines like an endless mesh of roads. . . .

"No," Lyolik says. "I left and that's that."

"I was afraid you wouldn't want to." Sam sighs. "They even wrote up an order. Look."

He pulls the order with its signatures and seals out of his bag.

But Lyolik still shakes his head no.

"No. They threw me away like a broken puppet."

"Oh, Lyolik!" Sam says, now utterly hopeless. "Everyone, everyone down to the last actor, asked me to tell you that they want you to come back. Even Filipp."

"They shouldn't have tossed me out." Lyolik purses his lips sternly. "Then they wouldn't have had to ask."

All of a sudden I burst.

I start talking — and can't stop.

About how Sashok and I sat in the puppet room over the drawings and how afraid we were to break the puppets — and not to break the puppets.

About asking their forgiveness.

About standing in the doorway to the puppet room when we heard a sound like nuts cracking.

About the theater dancing to jazz — even about the pilot at Baumanskaya whose knee I rubbed for luck.

I spill it all — and fall silent.

Then Lyolik stands up and goes to the vestibule — to put on his coat.

◈

That evening is like my birthday.

Or New Year's. Or my birthday and New Year's rolled into one.

There's so much joy inside me, I think I might float to the ceiling like a balloon.

Lyolik and Filipp look like surgeons: They concentrate on gluing, cutting, and pulling tight, they open up the puppet heads and miraculously turn the pieces back into a single whole; they replace springs and refasten the eye and mouth hooks to the control rods. Meanwhile Sashok and I stand by, loyal assistants, and mix glue and hand them the parts they need.

Sam runs out to the store: "One foot here, the other foot there, it's time to open the Candy Puppet Show!" Once again the workshops smell of chocolate, crisp wafers, nuts, and berry caramels intermingled with wood shavings and starch.

The actors run into the workshop, grab the puppets that are ready, and fly back onstage in what seems like one continuous leap. Mama Carlo smiles happily.

The music rumbles, lifting us to the clouds; the artificial candles on the holiday tree flicker onstage; there's the smell of glue and lacquer, candies and the holiday; Sam turns the Nutcracker into a person, and the puppets act as if they really are alive.

And no one in the audience even guesses that just that afternoon they were all hanging lifeless with closed eyes and dead arms.

No one in the audience understands, probably, why at the curtain call, when all the actors are standing there, wearier than usual and happy, Sam suddenly drags out onstage a hook-nosed old man in glasses and a knit vest, who smiles in confusion and hides his hands behind his back like a child. Or why absolutely all the actors surround him and applaud him without stopping, so that the applause mounts, explodes up by the ceiling, and falls on the audience like invisible confetti.

In any case, the audience stands up and claps — they clap for Lyolik — until the light onstage goes out and the heavy velvet curtain falls.

VII

Always in Greasepaint

Sometimes the most remarkable time is when the show is over and the stage is just mine and Sashok's.

For instance, if it's *Karurman: The Black Forest*.

Tomorrow they're going to rehearse it again. They have to bring in another actor for Sam's part.

I never recognize Sam in the mask of Shurale, the forest demon, and it scares me every time: his warty chin, his gray wrinkly cheeks, and the terrible horn on his forehead.

"New parts, always new parts," Timokhin grumbles,

and he nods at Sam. "And it's all because of you. The same drag every day. I'm about to start dreaming my part!"

"Go on with you, Seryozh" — and Sam smiles. And Timokhin — reluctantly — smiles back, because that's the only thing that works with Sam.

After the performance, the kettles are boiling in the dressing rooms, everyone comes from their own dressing rooms into one, and Mama and Sam get out tea bags and cups from the drawers — everyone gets their own. Sam's has red polka dots, and Father Gapon's is dark blue and so dirty you can see the unwashed brown coffee ring even on the dark blue. Mama's and Papa's are identical — white with malachite checks, but Papa's cup handle is broken off. The actors change their clothes, spend a long time removing their makeup in front of the mirror, lifting their chins and aiming the light from the round light bulbs at their narrowed eyes, which makes their eyelashes seem longer, and dawdle over their tea. Someone's got a cake, and Sam's probably brought cream-filled doughnuts from the theater snack bar.

When you bite into the fluffy wall of cake, you think there's just emptiness with a light nutty flavor, but right away you taste the cool, lightly sweet-but-tart cream.

Once I ran down to the snack bar during intermission, and even though Nina Ivanovna, the snack bar lady, wanted to let me go to the head of the line, I honestly stood the whole fifteen minutes, until the first bell — that's how long the line was — and then carefully, so as not to drop them, carried a plate heaped with pastries down the hall. I set it down on Sam's table, and when the show was over and he ran all over the theater searching for whoever it was who gave him the doughnuts, I sat there quietly and didn't confess.

There wouldn't have been any point to confessing.

The theater is now definitely ours, our good old theater. Lyolik reigns in the workshops once more, and even Filipp doesn't seem out of place there. Only, something has changed in Sam's dressing room. I don't understand why, but I feel the change. Only when Sashok says "Dutch textbook" do I understand.

The tables are covered with thin notebooks called cue scripts, which have all the cues for supporting the puppet's arm or giving the actor a prop sword. There are black and white boxes of makeup that smell like sharp cheese. But Sam's Dutch textbook isn't on the table anymore. It used to lie right under the mirror, and it was already dog-eared, like an uncombed head of hair. When Sam had time, he would sit over the open textbook, clutching his head, covering his ears with his fingers, and moving his lips ever so slightly. If you looked closely, you could see his throat vibrating, and you could tell he was saying the Dutch words to himself.

Now there's no textbook on the table: Sam has taken it home.

◆

After *Karurman*, everyone goes to the dressing rooms. The mysterious black forest onstage won't get dismantled until tomorrow. Sashok and I can crawl into the huge foam tree stumps wrapped in gnarled roots, and from there, from inside, look at the stage through a window in the foam covered with netting (for breathing) and imagine we're actors. Or scramble across the huge foam vines, like tightropes, or take a flying leap at the foam backdrop entwined with braided branches.

Karurman is all soft, all black and brown and swampy.

"Ashes, ashes, we all fall down!" Sashok commands, and we fall backward into the cozy foam nest covered on all sides by soft vines hanging from grates. You can feel like a kid again. Like when you just lived without thinking whether you were one way or another.

"Listen, what's going on in school?" Sashok asks after she gets her breath back.

"What do you mean? School's the same as always. Only now, every time I see Anton, I think of my grandfather. And

110

about how, when we were little, my grandfather liked Anton so much.

" 'You hold on to him. He's a good boy, a proper boy,' my grandfather would say. Proper, improper — it's all so easy for him. Either you're proper or you're not. It made me feel even more that I wasn't quite the way I should be. Anton's the right kind, and grandfather's the right kind, and I 'wasn't really a success.'

"What he meant by 'success' I still don't know, but obviously Anton was a sure success, in my grandfather's opinion."

Here, onstage, Sashok and I are basically waiting for Sam so that we can learn how to do a handstand. He does it better than anyone, and he's the only one we can ask to teach us. Papa never has time; he's either running out for a smoke or talking histrionically in the dressing room about how "it's a mess everywhere!" Timokhin has gotten too fat, Father Gapon is lazy, and Sultanov doesn't have the patience, and anyway he's old.

"Listen," Sashok says all of a sudden. "What if the grown-ups suddenly find out you're gay, like Sam? Or you don't turn out at all the way they've hoped? They'll feel uncomfortable right off, as if you've changed. But really, you're just the same!"

Children are a medal for them, I think. A medal for everyone to see. Something to hang on your chest and be proud of. Show off. But you don't brag about ones like Sam. No one would understand. It would be better not to have children like that at all. There aren't many who can be proud of you just because you're a good person.

Sam nods as if he's read my thoughts and steps forward from the black velvet backdrop as if he's materialized out of it. He walks over to us and sits in the foam nest too, crossing his legs.

"It's out of helplessness. They think looking closely at a puppet is silly and looking at a person to see his soul rather than his blueprint is hard. That's why they latch on to what they're used to, what they understand. A man. A woman. It's simpler and not so scary. It's the only thing they can see from the outside, the only thing they can grab on to. So they do, as if it were a life preserver. They think if they jump inside a person they'll drown. I feel sorry for them."

They're afraid of jumping inside a person and drowning, I repeat to myself.

"How about it? Shall we give it a try?" Sam scrambles easily to his feet. A second before, he'd been sitting there Turkish-fashion and now he's standing. I could never do that in a million years.

"Let's give it a try." Sashok gives her kind permission.

And we push off, nearly tearing into the foam backdrop threaded with swampy brown vines, and do a handstand the way Sam shows us. Your legs fly up, nearly toppling you, and in the first instant you're very scared you won't keep your balance, that you'll fall and have no other choice but to land helplessly on your back, but your heels meet the soft wall and suddenly everything's fine. Now you just have to stand there and not let your arms buckle too soon, and Sam comes over and corrects your heels and lightly touches your ankles so you keep your legs together.

And then, when you're not afraid anymore, you can try it in the middle of the stage, without the safety wall. Sam's standing next to you and he's got his arms stretched out to support you if anything happens. And then you suddenly have your own personal wall inside you. You feel the tips of your shoes stretching skyward, to the floodlights on the ceiling. You've turned into a tree and you can just stand there forever because Sam is right by your side.

"I've decided not to sell my apartment," Sam says out of nowhere, when we've run out of strength for our handstands and Sashok and I have plopped onto the padded floor. And for some reason he looks up, to where the mesh-covered lights blaze in the ceiling.

"What do you mean you're not selling it? What about the buyer?"

"He came and I apologized and turned him down."

"You mean you're not leaving?" Sashok is stunned.

"No, no, I'm leaving," Sam says quickly. "Just not for good. Not forever. The worst thing is to leave forever, after all" — he pauses — "in general. The worst thing is that 'forever.' It happens anyway when you're not looking. But if you make that forever happen yourself . . . Basically" — Sam slaps his knee — "I'll be visiting when I have a break in the theater. To look in on Lyolik and not leave him without anyone checking in."

◆

There is school the next day.

In the school stadium the snow from two days before has turned into a hard crust — it rained overnight and by morning it was frozen.

The gym teacher huddles in his red tracksuit, but he still drives us on to run circles around the stadium. The sharp trill of his whistle is like a bird that's suddenly woken up. My feet slip on the smooth snow, and the scariest thing is falling. I hate running in the stadium. I'd rather stand on my hands for half an hour. But no one cares about that in gym. Run until you get a stitch in your side and your heart rises so high in your throat you think it might slip out if you open your mouth. Today I suddenly have a very good idea of what Sashok must feel.

I'm glad that after gym I'll be leaving the school for the theater. That's why I have to change fast, and now I'm trying not to talk with anyone in the changing room, especially Anton. I have no desire to know what they all think of me. And say about me.

I want to toss my pack on my back and slip out past Zhmurik and into the hall as fast as I can. I'm not anywhere near him, but for some reason husky Zhmurik suddenly takes a step toward me, as if he's about to attack me — and shoves me by the shoulder as hard as he can.

"Hey! Watch it! He shoved me," he sings out in a fake voice.

"Our Grisha the queer is a troublemaker," Botsman chimes in playfully. He's short and has a unibrow, and he shoves me too. So hard I nearly fly into Anton.

I lift my head and look into his eyes — I don't know why. Maybe I thought that if I looked into my old friend's eyes everything would instantly be all right.

We look at each other for a second, and I see his eyelashes tremble very slightly, and I wait — but for what?

Then he looks away, sticks his hand out affectedly, and says mincingly, "Ugh! How re-volt-ing you are!" And he shoves me in the chest. I probably could have shoved him back. Could have. And I could have socked Botsman in the face so that he'd remember it his whole life. My hands were trained. I probably could have, and like Sam — three against one.

But right then my insides start writhing and twisting, and I smile pathetically and bleat, "What's with you?" The Jester. The Jester making faces. The Jester prepared to fall on the floor and do anything to make them stop, but . . . But what? Do they pity me?

What do I need their pity for?

For the first time I feel like ripping the Jester out of me, tearing off the Jester's cap that has frozen solid to my head, even if it takes my hair with it, all of it even — and stand up straight and pay them back. Hit them as hard as I can. Even Anton — right in his smiling bully face.

But all I can do is bleat, "What's with you?" and they guffaw and toss me from one to the next, as if I were a lifeless puppet — a real Jester.

They toss me around until Anton butts me so hard I fly backward into the changing room doors.

My back strikes the door, it opens, and at the last moment I grab the doorframe to keep from flying headfirst into the tiled floor of the hallway.

An empty hallway that Sashok is walking down toward the changing rooms.

Sashok, who has never once been to my school and didn't even seem to know exactly where I go to school.

Actually, I don't recognize her right away.

I've never seen Sashok look like this.

She's put on some impossibly red coat and — for the first time ever — a skirt. A very short skirt. And boots. I didn't even know she had boots. She's also used gel on her hair to make it stand up as if she were a hedgehog — a very fashionable hedgehog. And she's lined her eyebrows, for some reason. And put on lipstick. If you look closely — mascara too. All this makes her look like a puppet. A very pretty puppet, of course.

All of them — Botsman, Anton, and Zhmurik — pour out after me into the hall and are now getting an eyeful of Sashok.

"Who've you come for, my beauty?" Botsman asks insolently, and he smiles — and when Botsman smiles, he looks like a bony, earless mutt baring his teeth: He's either going to bite or just give you a scare.

"Not you, little boy." Sashok cuts him off and arches her lined eyebrows as if playing a part known to her alone. "Here's who" — and she comes up so close to me, I can see that the little fool has also applied something white in the corners of her eyes.

"No stinkin' way," Anton says, and everyone looks at me.

With respect — for the first time.

Just because Sashok wearing makeup and a red coat has come by for me.

And all of a sudden I see it. All of a sudden I understand: "Greasepaint makes everything easy as pie. Smear it on, and you feel confident. Think not? Just try it."

They're all in greasepaint! It's easier for them that way. One day they all smeared on greasepaint and now they can't get along without it. Being themselves — without a made-up face that hides who you really are. That doesn't let you smile and cry when you want to, like you did when you were a kid. It doesn't let you be free.

I understand what Sam meant, and I start to feel sorry for them — Anton, Botsman, and Zhmurik. And my grandfather, who's in greasepaint too.

They're so easy to fool. That's why I feel sorry for them.

Sashok grabs me by the collar, pulls me toward her with a jerk, and presses her lips to mine. Her lips are as cold as a corpse's.

Anton, Botsman, and Zhmurik stare at us as if we're tigers in a circus ring.

Sashok pulls away slightly and whispers softly, "Look at me, idiot. Don't look to the side." And she sticks her lips to mine again.

And all of a sudden, for no reason at all, I realize that Sashok is a Jester too. Definitely. With an upturned crown on her head. And when you're a Jester — a real Jester, not like me, just making faces — you're more powerful than any king.

Then she pulls away and runs her finger across my cheek with a tenderness that doesn't suit her at all, shakes her nonexistent bangs, and looks triumphantly at the dumbstruck Anton.

She waves good-bye to the guys — "So long, boys!" — puts her arm around my waist, and leads me away.

The next day, Anton says with respect, "That's quite some girl you've got."

VIII

SALTY PEARS

REMEMBER the Jester puppet right before Sam leaves.

I realize it's been a week since the show's been decommissioned.

And the reason I remember is probably just that Sashok is spending less time at the theater now — going to pre-op appointments.

"Don't you get up to any tricks without me," she said in her funny way when she was leaving for her very first work-up, and she looked at me pretty seriously, her eyes turning the color of asphalt.

"She's waited a long time." I pat the gym bag at my side and go to the puppet room to pick up my Jester. Decommissioned already. So he'll become Sashok's Jester at New Year's. Maybe she'll even take him to the hospital. I imagine him sitting on the table by her bed, and if she ever wakes up in the night — it seems to me that people do wake up in the night in hospitals — she'll see the Jester's smile and be happy. And fall soundly back to sleep.

The door to the puppet room is open, as always, and you can skip across the threshold with a single bound and land imagining you're in a show onstage.

The imp with the red horns and stuck-out tongue, Lyudmila in her marsh-green dress, Losharik, the Hussar, and Hortensia and Javotta — Cinderella's stepsisters. Javotta, Hortensia, and Cinderella in a fancy gown. There are two Cinderellas in the show: one in a sacking cap and a dirty cotton dress, with soot stains on her cheeks; the other in a fancy white ball gown with the hem fastened to her elegant hand so you can see the tips of her glass slippers.

The King, the Queen, Cinderella in her ball gown, Hortensia, Javotta . . .

I keep counting and recounting them because it seems as though, if I count them again, they will show up, Cinderella in her sacking apron and the ever-smiling Jester.

But they're not here.

122

They've been hung somewhere else, I guess. That's it! Hung somewhere else!

Someone probably wants to take the Cinderella with the sooty cheeks home too. And they've hid them so no one else will take them.

When you climb up to the Roost, the steps shake and the railings hum lightly, and up top the prop fruits and weightless, fake farmers' yokes lie there deaf and dumb.

The Jester and Cinderella aren't here either.

"Are you playing a game?" Tanya the wardrobe mistress smiles good-naturedly and doesn't understand why I grab her hand.

"Tanya, have you seen the Jester? The one from *Slipper*? The one that was decommissioned?"

Tanya furrows her brow. "Ask Olezhek. I think he gave away some of the puppets."

My heart thuds to my feet, which are suddenly heavy and weak. You want to go somewhere, but can't.

For the very first time — even if my feet won't obey — I'm not afraid of going alone, without Sashok, straight to Olezhek's office. Running into him in the hall isn't scary, but going there as if he called you in is a very different thing. After all, in his office even Olezhek is a boss.

On the way, you suddenly notice everything you usually don't: a crack that runs the full length of the wall next to the staircase, a broken-off piece of marble stair, a forgotten pile of dusty trash in a corner. The letter *v* in "Kolokolchikov" on the door plaque seems to have swollen, as if from rain.

"Come in, kid!"

How does Kolokolchikov manage to seem to be looking at you and past you at the same time?

"What did you do with the Jester?" My palms start sweating, and, trying to look casual, I rest them on my jeans.

"The Jester? From *Slipper*, you mean?" Olezhek sounds surprised. "The day before yesterday he and Cinderella were taken into a private collection."

He says "private collection" in such a deferential way, you'd think it was some famous museum. And he adds, boasting, "Not every theater has its puppets bought by collectors, kid. Oh, no, not every theater."

He says it as if he personally had once made the Jester. And also, his crowning glory: "And now the money will go toward new puppets."

His voice rises like a rooster's, and you can hear how impossibly proud Olezhek is of himself.

My voice gets husky.

My voice gets hoarse.

I want my voice to be more persuasive, but it comes out just like some kid's.

"But you promised!" I say pathetically. "You promised me!"

Olezhek looks at me with sympathy.

"Really? Well, all right, kid. Go take any of the other ones left" — and he nods briefly, as if he's figured out how to feed all the hungry people of the world and is terribly pleased with himself. Like, "That's the way the cookie crumbles, kid. Go on, kid. This conversation's over, kid."

I leave Olezhek's office and don't even know where to go.

For some reason I go to the men's room the audience uses. I realize this is the wrong way. I wander to the street exit. Only at the exit do I realize it's cold. Snow is falling — stinging, more like sleet than snow.

Elokhovskaya Church doesn't look like a pinecone anymore.

It's ugly now.

Because Olezhek has given away my Jester to some collector, and now I have nothing to give Sashok. And no one is going to sit on her nightstand by her bed and smile at her if she suddenly wakes up in the night — and in hospitals people must always be waking up in the night.

Then I stop in my tracks, run all the way around the theater, and slip through the actor's entrance — and Albert Ilich stares and shakes his head when he sees my red hands. "Mad as hatters, these theater kids."

At first my hands are totally numb, then they feel as if they're being stung by a thousand needles, and then they're flooded with heat — as if I've spiked a very high fever.

Then I decide I can't leave it at this. First I decide to kill Olezhek. So he'll know.

So he'll know what happens when you make a promise and then do what he did. It's all Olezhek's fault! If not for him, I'd have the Jester in my bag right now — for Sashok.

Only, how can I kill him? How do you kill someone?

I pace and think — and just can't see me killing Olezhek.

Then I suddenly imagine telling Sashok this, in an ordinary voice, calmly — there, I killed Olezhek because he sold the Jester.

Only that won't bring the Jester back. Even if I kill Olezhek, it won't.

And I can't tell anyone about the Jester. After all, Sashok doesn't have to know the Jester isn't in the theater anymore. Especially since she's having her operation soon.

◆

When you keep something to yourself for a long time, it starts seeming as though no one cares about you, that they even set things up specially this way, so you'd be afraid to tell them everything.

New Year's is coming. Mama makes trips to some stores and comes back looking mischievous and saying, "Oh, my, I can barely drag my feet!" Papa is preparing for the holiday party — and so is everyone in the theater: Father Gapon, Timokhin, and even old Sultanov.

Holiday trees are a big deal at New Year's, and before the holidays it seems to me there are more trees in Moscow than children.

Papa is learning the part of Father Frost, so the whole apartment is littered with pages from scripts. Mama goes into the attic and takes out an antique suitcase with tooled leather corners. I know what's in the suitcase, of course: a dark blue, full-length fur coat with silver snowflakes, a matching cap, and a white beard.

Mama spends a long time cleaning the coat and beard and yelling at Papa: "You're as lazy as your mother! You could have washed this makeup off a year ago. Now it's all stuck on! You can go to the devil with your beard now." She doesn't mean anything of the kind, of course. She'll comb out the beard to make it fluffy.

And by New Year's Papa will lose his voice because he's been moonlighting, Father Frost-ing from school to school and kindergarten to kindergarten and using his voice improperly, not the way they were taught at the theatrical institute, and he'll lose his voice, and Mama will say contemptuously,

"Mr. Fine Actor, the unlucky hack." And he will just croak, "You be quiet" — and she'll wave her hand at him.

Everyone has holiday trees. Or presents. Even the round lights in the metro look like big tree ornaments. The only thing on anyone's mind is the holidays.

Except for me. The only thing on my mind is the Jester.

Eventually I realize that if I don't tell someone about the Jester, and very soon, I'll burst like a fine glass ornament dropped on a tile floor. I'll shatter in every direction, and that's all there is to it.

"I can steal it," I tell Sam. I don't care that Filipp is sitting right there. "I'll find the collector's address in Olezhek's office and steal it. That would be the right thing. Or something else. Sort of like that."

Sam looks at me and says nothing. Nothing. And I feel myself getting smaller and smaller inside.

But I don't want to be smaller. I'm angry. At myself and Sam. I'm just about to shout something awful at him: "It's fine for you. You're so perfect. You're leaving the day after tomorrow anyway, and you don't understand anything!"

I'm about to open my mouth to blurt that out and see if his face changes from hurt.

But instead, for some reason, I say, "Well, it's not as though I can make another Jester — for Sashok! A new one. Just the same."

"No?" is all Sam says. "No?"

I get very hot. And then very cold.

Because that scares me.

Because it turns out that deciding to break a puppet isn't nearly as scary as deciding to make one myself. In horror, I mumble, "Well, even if I could . . . what about the cap . . . I could never sew the cap myself."

◆

Sam leaves during the evening performance. "Bye!" he says, and he smiles so hard his dimple shows. And he raises his hand in salute, as always. Only the fact that he's taking a suitcase is unusual.

"Why so few things?" Sashok wonders, touching the new tag with Sam's name — unrecognizable, because it's so unlike our real life.

Even the address — the tag has a strange address, written in a strange way, and below, in English, "Holland."

And because of that, both the suitcase and everything else seem unreal — because Sam is the same.

He smiles the same way: with his eyebrows, eyelashes, almost alien cheekbones, and even the lobes of his neat ears. He tosses his long white scarf just as nonchalantly over his shoulder.

"I sent the rest on ahead," he explains to Sashok.

Then Sam drinks tea with everyone in the changing room and runs off to see Lyolik and joke with Mama Carlo. He's waiting for the third bell and all the actors to take their puppets off the wooden rack and run out onstage.

"You should do it. You've already decided," he says in parting.

He gives me a hug. And in the second my cheek brushes his rough cheek I'm able to smell — and remember for a long time — the smell of Sam's cheek: the salty sea and pears, for some reason.

I don't watch him walk away, pulling his dark blue suitcase like a fat dog. I hate watching people walk away. I just sit down on a step of the iron staircase leading to Maika and the sound men so that all I can hear is the music from the stage. The old theater sighs sadly, its slender railings shuddering under my palms.

"Kurskaya . . . Taganskaya . . . Paveletskaya . . ." Sashok says at five-minute intervals, tapping her finger for each metro station Sam might be passing through right then.

I really want to tell her to shut up, but I don't. I myself would be repeating the names of the streets if I could swallow my heart, which gets stuck at every breath.

I imagine Sam sitting in the airplane and watching the MOSCOW sign glowing purple and the white snow moths whizzing around in the light of the airport's dandelion floodlights. And the cars and trucks crawling across the airfield like beetles with Russian signs on their snowy white sides.

Then he'll skip over the forests and rivers and the country houses below, and lots and lots of towns — some bigger, some smaller — and see more beetle-cars crossing airfields, and you can tell, even in the darkness, that the writing on them is in different, foreign letters.

Sam will continue on, taking a taxi through the nighttime city, and the wet snow will turn into autumn rain on the windshield, and the taxi's dashboard will glow green in the dark. And then Sam might press his round forehead to the tear-stained glass — like me and Sashok that time in the metro — and get to thinking about the last bell before the start of the show, about Lyolik's gnarled hands and the Jester's smile, about the polka dot cup filled with freshly brewed tea during intermission, and about all the bustle. Sam may even get to thinking about Kolokolchikov there, in Holland.

And about me.

IX

The Jester's Cap

WHEN it lies idle, it's stiff, firm, and dry. In short, dead. I take the old pieces of modeling clay, which are all different colors and don't look very good, and hold them in my hot hands. Then the pieces come to life. They become soft and warm. They breathe. They lie down on each other like petals, like patches, and when you smooth them and pinch them they are softer than silk. They aren't stiff, ugly pieces anymore; they're transformed into a clay sphere in your hands, into a warm, smooth sphere.

And it seems to me that I'm holding the whole Earth in my hands, the whole past and future, and there, inside, is everyone who has sculpted puppet heads like this before me.

Light from the street comes streaming through the window. Outside, the streetcars are running down the rails and glowing in the dark blue winter's evening, like magic boxes. Millions of little lamps flood and sparkle on the pre-New Year's side streets, and light from the holiday garlands fills the room.

I am standing there, and in my hands is a head. What will be a head. The most important part of a puppet.

Mama always said I had talent; she always said one day I'd sculpt something. I don't know what it feels like when you have talent. I am just holding a warm clay sphere, and lying on the table are very old drawings, yellowed with time, which Lyolik has found for me in the heat-cracked cupboards. From the drawings, which smell like ancient books, the Jester looks at me — full face and in profile.

I'm holding a smooth sphere, and you could toss it up and juggle it, as if you were in a circus, you could put it on the table, and you could sculpt a jester's head. My fingers touch the modeling clay and they know, they can feel it. Press here for the eye sockets and here for the hooked nose. The drawing on the table flows into my hands like languid music, and my hands repeat all the bends and curves of the Jester's face. They gently pull out the nose, and with a light movement, as if chopping down a sapling, they mark the arched brows, and then the fingers pinch out the clay and then smooth down the sharp cheekbones and the nose's hook.

I am holding a head, and there is already a hint of the Jester's crooked grin, and that makes me feel uneasy.

Now for the very hardest part. Now I have to cut the clay head in half, to make it easier to glue on the paper for the papier-mâché. Cut the face from top to bottom, straight through the forehead and nose. Lyolik does this with a sharp wire with handles on either end for easier holding. He calls it his string. I do the same, of course. I don't know any other way. Lyolik lent me his string. "Don't break it," he said, and he looked over his glasses and suddenly smiled because how could anyone break it? There's nothing to break.

Cutting the face is scary too, because the Jester is almost there already. What if you spoil something, something there's still no trace of?

Neatly put the clay head on the old oak partition, which smells like the storeroom, hold the slender handles, stretch the wire as far as it will go, take aim, and then plunge the string like a knife into the soft modeling clay, and, not believing your luck, not believing it worked, cautiously separate the round, knobby head into two halves. And you think: It's just like an apple cut by a knife, just exactly like an apple.

In the little room behind the workshops the world seems to have shrunk to the size of the table and the window opening on the square.

"You really want to work there?" Lyolik asked immediately when he learned about the Jester.

I didn't know that another work station could be set up behind the small door, in the little storeroom.

It's calmer working around Lyolik and Mama Carlo.

I know they are there if anything happens. I know I have to make the Jester myself, alone, no matter what. Still, it's more peaceful being next to them.

Sometimes Mama Carlo pokes her head through the doorway and says, "Time for tea," and then I suddenly realize that this time I didn't even hear her put on the water or brew the tea.

I come out of my room, and it feels like surfacing from incredible depths where absolutely everything is different. Only the theater reminds me that it's the same. Its heavy door shifts behind me, protecting me; its creaking floorboards whisper something, and it murmurs — but I have no time to listen.

"Are you going to make it from papier-mâché?" Filipp asks skeptically after examining my modeling clay pieces, which lie cut-side down on the table like two apple halves. "I'd have carved them from wood. Wood is nobler."

That gets to me. "Go carve them yourself! Only do it yourself, get it?"

Before, I probably wouldn't have said anything, but this time I flare up. Once you've sculpted a puppet head yourself, everything changes.

"What's with you? I was just saying," he fusses. "Do it your way. You're the boss here." He falls silent, looking at the modeling clay halves of the Jester's head. "If anything comes up, I'll help. If you want." And he hurriedly repeats, "You know, if you want."

"I do," I blurt out, to my own surprise. "Only, just a little."

"You're definitely going to need lead," Filipp adds pragmatically. "Otherwise the puppet won't move well. Lead in the chin and lead in the backside, so his posture is right, lead in the hands and feet, in the heels, so the boots don't point down and the puppet walks like a person. Definitely."

"Thank you," I manage to get out. For some reason it's very hard for me to say thank you, especially to Filipp. He's a complete mystery to me, and I never know what to expect from him.

"Nutcase. Nothing to it!" Filipp says with a wave of his hand, casually, and his skinny shoulder jerks, and his tattooed dragon winks its round eye at me.

Filipp focuses on laying out lead weights on the table. "This for the chin, this for the hands, this . . ."

I can't stop myself: "Listen, there's something I don't get. Why are you doing this? Why should you help?"

Filipp suddenly raises his eyes — which are very blue, it turns out — in surprise, as if he hasn't expected such foolishness from me. And then, as if to say, *Why am I even confiding in you?* he grins, and the tidy beard under his lower lip shifts to one side.

"I'm a selfish pig!" he says defiantly. "A pig, see? I thought I'd get some practice in at the same time, on your Jester, like a lab animal. It's not like making puppets for a show. If it doesn't work out, it's no tragedy."

And for some reason, I don't believe him.

You're always lying, I think. I'd swear to it. You're lying!

But Filipp, noticing, probably, that I don't much believe him, adds passionately, "Why do you think I said that about the puppets? Why did I take all the blame? You think I'm good? Like hell. I'm a selfish beast." He seems to like calling himself a beast an awful lot, and he blinks with satisfaction.

"Why *did* you say that? You could have kept it to yourself."

"I wanted Lyolik to come back too. Only not like you did. Differently. I wanted someone to teach me to make puppets unlike anyone else's. And only Lyolik can do that. I need a teacher and that's it. No charity whatsoever. None whatsoever."

His eyebrows are dancing and his eyes are squinting so much that fine wrinkles form around his eyes like sunbeams and the dragon on his shoulder wiggles its black mustache menacingly.

And all of a sudden I understand.

I'm delighted, as if I've run into an old friend on the street, an old friend I haven't seen in a very long time.

I understand that Filipp is a Jester too.

◆

True masters do their papier-mâché over plaster, not modeling clay.

They cast plaster forms from the head halves and paste the paper on the inside. Then, when the halves are still a little damp, you have to carefully pull them out of the plaster carcasses and secure them to the table with tacks, so that when the papier-mâché dries, there's no shrinkage. "Don't pull," Filipp says, explaining it all to me. He isn't being mean. I really would have pulled. After all, you have to make more than one puppet for it to come out right. That's why I'm doing my Jester the simple way, pasting over a modeling clay half.

Vaseline cools your hands. You can scoop it out, lay it on the halves of the Jester head in big swipes, spread it out, and cover every millimeter of the clay. You breathe in the smell of vanilla and powder.

You have to have the Vaseline or else you'll never pull the clay halves away from the papier-mâché.

When you're cooking the glue, you feel like a wizard. You sprinkle in the flour and mix it with cold water for a very long time, until you feel as if you're not here anymore but somewhere else — and you see the water and flour turn into a thick white gel. You pound pieces of wood glue and pour water over them, like a real chef, and you put the old pot on the fire, the pot where Lyolik makes his glue. The pot has deep dents on the sides. How many puppets has it helped make in its day? On the burner, the pot dances from the heat, as if it wants to run away from the old burner. Then you mix your flour paste with the wood glue, which is as thick as porridge, and it doesn't seem all that hard, making puppet flesh out of flour and water.

You soak pieces of newspaper in the glue and overlap them on the convex clay head halves. Over and over you smooth out the wrinkles with your finger and then you lay down more and more, over the hooked nose and the eye sockets, on the forehead and the bumpy cheeks, hearing and seeing nothing but the Jester's head growing millimeter by millimeter.

Lyolik teaches me how to tell when the papier-mâché has dried through — and the next time I come back to the theater, I lightly flick a face half. It clinks very slightly, the way only dry papier-mâché can clink. Then you can place the apple halves back together, cut off the extra pieces of papier-mâché, and glue both halves together.

The Jester. There he is: the Jester.

The finished head still has to be pasted over with newspapers, but the most important part seems done.

"You're lucky," Filipp says with irony. "Lyolik has plenty of arm and leg pieces; you won't have to sweat away at those."

On the other hand, I have to make the crossbar you hang the Jester on for him to come to life. I sit over the drawings for hours. I cut out paper patterns, which I lay down on the thick veneer, and draw around them neatly so as not to be off by a single millimeter. I saw out the crossbar's details: the yoke for the arms and legs, which goes into the base, like the pieces of a construction set. I sweat and worry inside because I'm so afraid of making a mistake and ruining everything.

My head is filled with nothing but controllers. I am calculating where to drill the holes for the strings to make the hanger brackets for the arms and legs.

In math class I imagine how the Jester is going to move if I hang him just right. I move my fingers imagining him taking a step and waving his arm.

"Lost in nirvana?" Anton teases, and he elbows me in the side as hard as he can.

And then, for the first time, the jester in me — the one that's always inside me, the one that makes humiliating faces — disappears. Suddenly I can be myself, without being embarrassed or hiding.

"Drop dead!" I burst out, and I elbow him back.

He looks at me in amazement, as if seeing me for the first time, and so as not to appear the loser — Anton hates losing more than anything — he jokes, "Grishka bites!"

"Yes," I say, so loudly that everyone turns around. "Yes, I do now. And, basically, this is all so pathetic. You used to be interesting, Anton, and now you're boring."

He looks at me steadily. "Idiot!" The math teacher moves toward us like an overloaded ship.

"Anton, go out in the hall this minute!" she declares loudly. "I'll teach you to interrupt my class!"

"It's not me, it's Grishka," Anton sasses back, slumping in his chair.

The math teacher looks at me in surprise. But I just don't care — and that's why I stand up, feeling that the jester hunch on my back is gone, my back is straight, and now it's going to be just as straight as Sam's when he dances onstage.

"Well, yes, it was me, Maria Mikhailovna. And I'll go out into the hall." Botsman, Zhmurik, Anton, and everyone else look at me wide-eyed, as if they don't recognize me. The only jester inside me now is the true Jester, who is more powerful than kings. I nod in jest to Anton — "See you later, your highness" — and I walk past Botsman, past Zhmurik, and through the quiet class, open the door to the hall, and know that behind my back Anton is pale as a ghost and distraught, like a little boy who doesn't know what to do with his mama's favorite teacup, which he's accidentally broken.

Then I just collect my things in the cloakroom. I don't care what my teacher — or the principal — is going to say. I'm on my way to the theater, to finish the Jester.

"You're early today!" Filipp grins.

"Uh-huh," I say honestly. "I ran away from school. Listen, I keep wanting to ask you. Why do you need all these puppets anyway? With your father, you could work any-where you like."

Filipp eyes me for a moment, as if checking to see whether I'm being serious or not.

"You're just like my dad. He wanted to ship me off somewhere. As far away as possible. To England, for instance. So I wouldn't fool around." Filipp suddenly catches himself. "No, I have a world-class father. Especially when he forgets he's a boss. If he weren't world-class, I damn sure wouldn't have ended up here. One day I told him, 'No, I want to make puppets and that's it. I don't want to be a lawyer or a diplo-mat.' He nearly died. He shouted, 'You idiot, you'll be working as a security guard in a supermarket.' He wouldn't talk to me for a week. He was hoping I'd come around. Or get scared. But I started looking into theater studios. And he gave in. Another father wouldn't have."

Filipp smiles crookedly and strokes an old control rod, lying all alone on the windowsill. "That's why I'm frittering my life away here." He smiles, probably so I won't forget that he's a jester too, in fact.

Sometimes Lyolik hoists himself out of his armchair and comes into my corner. He looks closely at my Jester, turns it around, glances briefly at the old drawings, and then his crooked finger, which looks like an old tree knot, points to a spot on the drawings visible to him alone, and he says, "Reinforce it here, otherwise it won't hold up." After these words of Lyolik's I suddenly see something I haven't seen before. Something I haven't understood before.

I am still scared to smooth the finished head. I take the file from Lyolik and run it over the Jester's forehead with the deep wrinkle, over the cheeks, and over the hooked nose. The head rustles and sputters — and you can see all the uneven spots being filed down. It's pleasant once you're polishing the face and brow with sandpaper; you're not so scared you're going to break everything.

"The minute you start making a puppet, it ceases to be yours," Lyolik always says. I've never understood what he was talking about. "You can create your own puppet world, and you can populate it however you like, but beyond that it's out of your hands. The moment you conceive of a puppet, it's no longer yours. It belongs to itself."

Only now do I understand what Lyolik is always talking about.

I hold the Jester's finished head in my hands and I can feel that he is his own self. I'm only here to make him the way he wants to be.

I cook the gesso primer for the Jester's face and skin, so he'll come out the way he should, so he'll be easier to draw on. Filipp is standing over my shoulder. He dips his fingers in the warm glue, folds them in a mysterious gesture, and immediately opens them. "Not enough glue," he says, and he shakes his head. Then I add glue and cook it some more, and then I stir crushed chalk into the mix, and it starts looking like very thick sour cream. This is going to be the puppet face, and I'm going to paint it the way Sam painted his own face before every show.

The Jester is starting to look more and more like himself.

So am I. Somewhere inside, I too am becoming more and more like myself. Because until you've made a puppet, you're not the real thing.

◆

I never thought a face and Jester's cap would be nearly impossible. A face is a face; it's always there. And the cap's just a cap, an upturned crown with bells. Only now, all of a sudden, it turns out that you can't, you can't paint the face. After all, it's so easy to turn a puppet into a monster; you just have to draw its eyes wrong.

Or its eyebrows. Or pick up a brush, dip it in the carmine paint, and boldly run it along where the Jester's smiling teeth should be.

"A puppet never forgives hack work," Lyolik always says. It doesn't forgive hack work.

I sit down at the table a few times, prepare my paints and brushes — and simply can't bring myself to make the first stroke. As if with one single stroke I could kill the Jester forever.

"Help?" Filipp finally takes pity on me.

He straddles a stool, leans over the papier-mâché, dips a brush in the paint, and lightly runs it over the puppet's still-eyeless face. He seems to be touching the head with a magic wand because all of a sudden the cheekbones emerge and shadows lie on the nostrils — and the Jester begins to breathe. A dimple appears on his chin and a smile line on his cheek.

And then, when Filipp has stained all his fingers with paint and picked up the Jester's head to make it easier to work, the Jester suddenly opens his eyes. Now he's a real Jester, just the same as the one Olezhek gave to the unknown collector.

"But I'm taking a pass on the cap," Filipp says. "Try it yourself. Or come up with something instead of it. Just put some kind of cap on him."

✦

"How's your bird doing in there?" I ask Sashok, listening to her concentrated wheezing over the phone.

147

"I'm sick of it already!" she responds.

I should have gone long ago to see her in the hospital where she's waiting for her operation. "When are you going to visit Sashok?" Mama kept asking. But I kept putting off the moment. I don't know why.

Maybe because I wanted to show up with the Jester and see her surprise. And then I'd tell her the whole story from beginning to end. And I'd add — *I'm sorry, Sashok, I just couldn't get the cap right. What kind of puppet master am I, anyway? I'm sorry, Sashok. I really did want to sew a cap, but I don't know how. I tried, and there were lots of nights I couldn't get to sleep because I was thinking about what to do. And never came up with anything.*

"Will you come visit me?" she asks me all of a sudden, desperately.

And she falls silent, as if everything in the world now depends on me.

"I'll come, Sashok, I'll come," I reply hurriedly. "I'll bring you a present for your birthday. You're going to have the best present ever. From me. I'm going to make it."

"You fool," Sashok concludes joyfully, and she laughs.

◆

The needle pricks my fingers. "Use the thimble," Mama Carlo keeps growling. "You've completely maimed yourself."

The thimble is steel, and if you put it on your index finger, then you can't feel the softness of the silk scraps you're sewing together for the Jester's clothes. Cornflower blue scraps, crimson scraps, scraps the color of gooseberries.

"Before, Jesters wore only two colors," Lyolik says. "Black and white. Like day and night."

I cut diamonds out of the different colors of silk and sew them to one another with tiny, very tiny stitches, the way Mama Carlo shows me. The seams look almost like straight paths in an invisible forest. I smooth the small seams on the inside, like Filipp said. I'm learning how to hold an iron properly — and the details that made no sense yesterday are transformed into pants and a jacket. I thread a needle with red-edged silk to give the Jester a fancy collar. And the world seems to have turned into the multicolored scraps of the Jester's costume. The world is in color, of course, not black and white at all. Not like day and night.

I have to dress the arms and legs separately and then attach them to the Jester's body. Out of nothing, someone suddenly appears. He hatched, formed out of small parts — the foot in the painted wooden boot, the pink hand, and the shoulder hinge. He is still stiff, the Jester. He still can't walk and run, wave his hand, nod his head, or land onstage after a graceful leap. I need to teach him all that — so I attach the strings to the invisible hooks on the Jester's body, hooks

I spent two whole evenings screwing in. As soon as a string is attached and secured to the opening in the controller, it comes to life. It vibrates and sings. It trembles as if someone has just awakened it, rescuing it from a long sleep.

I lift the controller, and the string-sinews shudder as they take on the Jester's weight, and he jerks, trying to get up.

"Something's come for you!" Mama Carlo trumpets — and she waves a thin, grayish piece of paper in the air.

Something's come? At first I don't understand that I've been sent a package. Or a packet. Or a letter. Like a grown-up would get.

"Let's go pick it up," Mama Carlo suggests, and she straightens her suspenders, wraps herself up like a cabbage in an old woolen top, and slaps on her knit cap with the awful little pompons. "I have to go to the store anyway."

The package was sent to the theater, Mama Carlo says, but addressed to me. I can't pick up packages at the post office myself yet because I'm not old enough, so I'm glad someone is going with me. Someone none other than Mama Carlo.

She takes long, almost soldierly strides and avoids the sidewalk curbs, the islands of ice, and all the frozen steps at once. She digs around in her bag and takes out her dark red passport and the postal notification. Then my co-conspirator nods to the fat postal worker in the window, who smells of borscht and fresh, spongy black bread, and with a broad, almost regal gesture, signs for receipt.

Then she says nasally, "Well, can you get back yourself? I still have to go to the store."

Because of the box, which I can only carry wrapped in my arms, I can't see my feet, so I walk cautiously, with tiny little steps.

The air suddenly smells of the New Year and tangerines — and as if someone has pulled an enormous Christmas cracker up above and snow is falling out of it like white confetti. It's falling in giant, fluffy flakes, so big they look like stage props. The snow falls in a small drift on the big box. I quickly pull my hand away and very quickly, so as not to drop my package, brush off the newly fallen snow. I can see the apple-red circles, the tulip-shaped symbol in the crown of a foreign post, and the theater's address printed in Latin letters. And my name, which Sam has written.

I don't even want to try to guess what's there, inside, even though I'm terribly curious. I just walk along quietly for fear of frightening off my joy that Sam hasn't forgotten me.

It feels as though he's smiling at me from far away, that I can see the dimple in his cheek and him waving to me — greetings, greetings. I smile back at Sam, and my mouth spreads wide, from ear to ear, as if stitched in place.

The Jester is waiting for me in the room with the view of the square. He too is probably curious to see what has come from Sam. He's sitting on the table, his back leaning against the wall, and the light of the streetlamps falls on the knees of his multicolored pants. The Jester looks like an ice angel, as if he's about to snap his strings and fly off, or break from a careless movement because he's so fragile. Only his smile — his rascally smile — says, "What angel? No one's breaking me."

Tomorrow I'll take him to Sashok so that he can guard her in the night.

But for now — see, Jester? — I take the big scissors and slit open the orange box. I take out the inflated packing pillows and pull off the thick wrapping paper. Then I start to see the scraps and bells — cornflower blue and crimson scraps, and even that familiar scrap the color of gooseberries.

All new, brilliant, and elegant. A Jester's cap.

More Powerful Than a King

I GO to see Sashok immediately after her operation — I'm almost the first. The Jester and I. We go together.

Lyolik taught me the best way to carry a marionette in a bag. You have to take all the strings in your hand and wind them tightly around the controller, like a hank, so they don't get tangled and break by accident.

I wrap the Jester in a flannel blanket — only his nose sticks out — and I keep thinking he's going to freeze before we get to Sashok.

I think about Sam all morning.

What he'll say when he sees the Jester. How he'll smile. How he'll take up the controller and lead him across the floor, as if he were alive. How he'll run his tapered, olive-skinned fingers over all the controller's levers like piano keys.

I examine the bright scraps of the Jester's cap and imagine Sam, far away, choosing them. Or ordering them. And when I picture him tilting his head and the wrinkles fanning out around his smile, I don't feel so sad.

♦

"Why the long face, Grigory?" my grandfather asks too cheerfully, and he claps me on the shoulder with his firm hand.

Every time my grandfather comes over, he asks me the same thing. "Why so sad?" or "Why so gloomy?" or "What are you smiling at, Grigory?"

As if he doesn't know what else to say. I never know what to answer, so I just say, "Nothing, I'm fine."

Then my grandfather immediately turns away, as if I've said some magic word and now he can go calmly about what he's been doing and ignore me.

Only, that "Nothing, I'm fine" is a lie. And I don't want to lie anymore.

"Why the long face, Grigory?" my grandfather says too cheerfully today. He's already getting ready to turn around, anticipating the usual "Nothing, I'm fine," but I suddenly say, "I miss Sam."

My grandfather's face turns to stone.

"Don't make things up" is all he can say. And he frowns.

"I'm not making things up," I answer defiantly. I'm not going to cave to him anymore. "I'm not making things up. I really do miss him."

I see my grandfather getting angry — because he doesn't know what to do.

"Don't make things up," he repeats, now angrily. "Don't pretend you miss some queer."

Rage surges and washes over me like a wave, blinding and deafening me.

"He's not a queer! He's a human being!" I shout. "The best person in the world!"

My grandfather turns red. "Human beings are human beings. And queers are queers. Perverts."

"You're the pervert!" I scream as loud as I can, not believing it's me screaming. That I've dared stand up to my grandfather. And that now I'm my own person and I think nothing of his contempt.

That what is said is more powerful than what isn't.

"And if that's true, then I'm a queer. Go on, say it! Say it! Say 'queer' to me!"

"You're lying!" My grandfather is totally red.

"I'm not lying!" I shout in reply and I feel myself turning red too.

"You're lying, you swine!" my grandfather shrieks almost like a woman, and he hauls back and takes a swing at my face. He misses my cheek, but his hard hand brushes my brow and temple, and my skin bruises immediately, as if it's been swiped by the sandpaper for polishing papier-mâché.

I don't notice Mama coming into the room.

"You hit him," she says to my grandfather in a calmly sinister voice. "Apologize this minute."

My grandfather stares at her.

"You too? You know everything? You're the one who spoiled him. He was a normal kid! Filth! Abomination! Perversion! This is your fault. You're the one who threw your child at that theater queer!" My grandfather looms over Mama like a mountain ready to come crashing down on her.

He shouts, paying no attention to me standing in the room, as if he even likes it that I shrink, as if he is giving me a good thrashing.

"This is a disease. Do you understand?" he shouts. "He needs treatment! Treatment! This can be treated!"

My grandfather doesn't look at me at all, and even I begin to wonder whether I'm here or not.

Suddenly I understand Sam perfectly, to the tips of my toes. I feel the loneliness he must have woken up with in the morning and fallen asleep with at night, a tremendous loneliness that never goes away, even if there are plenty of people all around you.

"It's you who needs treating," Mama says quietly, and she turns completely white. "You're attacking your grandson. That's it. We have nothing to talk about."

"Fool! Fool! You've always been a fool!" My grandfather's shouts get louder and louder, as if he's afraid he can't outshout Mama's quiet voice.

"Don't be expecting any grandchildren!" My grandfather spits out the words spitefully. Then he checks himself. "I should talk. I did, but I wish I'd never had a grandson."

He turns around and walks out.

And slams the door so that the teacups tinkle delicately and plaintively in the cupboard.

And a silence falls: a strange, resounding silence. Mama looks past me.

"He'll be back. Probably," she says without confidence.

I walk over to her and just push my forehead into her shoulder. One day I'll grow up. I'll grow up and I won't cry. Ever.

♦

The crunching, frosty morning has turned the city into a New Year's scene. The tree branches under the hospital window line the sky with black strokes, as if all this were a shadow theater, and the azure and yellow tomtits in the snow look like fluffy holiday tree ornaments.

In the long gray corridor I unwrap the flannel blanket, and the Jester splashes cornflower blue, gooseberry purple, and apple red. He laughs, and the hospital walls turn into multicolored screens, into a nice new backstage, into artificially lit fire gratings.

He has to see everything, so I sit him on my shoulder, and for a second it feels as though Sam is nearby.

I take his hand in mine, his smooth, comfortable hand, as if it isn't wooden at all, and it rests quietly in my hand.

It's a strange thing. I've always thought that Sashok was much older and stronger than me. But today I feel older and stronger than her — stronger than everyone. Even my grandfather.

The Jester seems to lightly put his heel forward: Come on, go, forward.

And he — no, I — open the door and see the hospital ward with the bright green walls and the IV drip stretching like a fine marionette string to the bed and the familiar shorn head.

"Hi, Sashok!" I shout straight from the threshold, and she smiles broadly, so broadly she doesn't seem sick at all. And then I suddenly see how pretty she is, even in the hospital, and that her lips aren't bluish but alive and warm, and inside me, heat spreads from somewhere in my core.

"Hi! The Jester and I have come to see you."

DARIA WILKE was born in Moscow in 1976, and drew on her childhood while writing this novel, as she grew up in a family of puppeteers. She now works at the University of Vienna in Austria.

MARIAN SCHWARTZ is an award-winning translator of classic and contemporary Russian literature. She is the recipient of two National Endowment for the Arts translation fellowships and is a past president of the American Literary Translators Association. She studied Russian at Harvard University, Middlebury Russian School, and Leningrad State University, and received a master's from the University of Texas at Austin. She lives in Austin, Texas.

This book was edited by Emily Clement and designed by Sharismar Rodriguez. The text was set in Spectrum MT, a typeface designed by Jan van Krimpen. The book was printed and bound at R. R. Donnelley in Crawfordsville, Indiana. Production was supervised by Starr Baer, and manufacturing was supervised by Shannon Rice.